# DRIVEN WILD BY THE GRIZZLY

## OBSESSED MOUNTAIN MATES

### ARIANA HAWKES

**Imprint:** Independently published

**ISBN:** 9798859388998

**Cover art:** Thunderface Design

**www.arianahawkes.com**

*Jessica*

*W*hine... *rattle... grrrr!*
        *Holy moly.* I'll be lucky if this poor old bus makes it up the mountain in one piece. The driver keeps grinding the gears, but it's going slower and slower, like some ancient beast on its last legs—uh, wheels.

I puff out my cheeks and stare through the window at a bunch of gnarly-looking pine trees. I've been sitting here for an hour already. Honestly, it'd be faster to walk right now. Maybe I should do that. Take some of the load off, anyway.

*No, Jessica, that's a ridiculous idea. What if it gets to the top of the hill and takes off without you?*

*You'll be screwed, that's what.*

I just need to stay put and deal with it. This is what

happens when you don't have a car. You take the public, hundred-year-old bus service and hope for the best. It's already stopped a bunch of times to let people off, and now I'm alone on the back seat. Just me and the driver, hauling ass up the mountainside.

I don't think the bus driver is too happy about being here, either. He keeps growling out a bunch of what I'm pretty sure are NSFW cusswords, and rolling his shoulders—which are massive and tattooed, by the way. I've only seen his back view so far, because I entered via the rear doors, but he's kind of scary-looking. He's wearing a wife beater, and his dark hair is swept up in a man bun. Nothing like a typical bus driver. Not that I'm an expert on bus drivers.

Well, as long as he gets me back to Twin Falls some time before midnight, that's the main thing.

To be honest, I'm not in a big hurry to get home and give my brother the 'good news'.

I let out a loud groan. I can do that, since I'm all alone back here. And it makes me feel a little better.

Seriously, do I have a sign on my forehead saying, *weirdos, losers and psychopaths welcome here?*

This morning, I woke up all excited. I was about to start my dream apprenticeship, working for this guy who's basically a god in the jewelry-design world. But let's just say, he's not the person I thought he'd be. I wound up hightailing it out of his workshop, all the way back to the darn bus stop. And now I'll have to tell my brother what happened, and he's going to be so mad. We already had to move towns after a guy I was dating turned into a crazed stalker, and got all, *if I can't have you, no one will.*

My brother, Ricky, is a great guy, but he's been struggling to get his auto repair business started up again in a new town and it's stressing him out. We were so relieved when I landed this paid apprenticeship. But now I'll have to find some other work, A-sap. And probably give up on my dream of being a jewelry designer.

I press my forehead to the cold windowpane, replaying this morning's episode. Wondering if it was something I did, or said. Ricky told me it wasn't my fault that my ex went psycho. But what's that old saying? *Once is unlucky, twice is...*

*Grrr!* The bus's engine gets even louder and we break above the tree line, and... wow. Until now, we'd been passing through an area of dense forest, but now daylight floods the interior of the bus. We're up high on a mountain peak, and the view is incredible. Little wisps of cloud are floating past the windows, while down below the valley unfolds in a patchwork of fields and vegetation. I can just make out a cluster of houses far, far away, which might be Twin Falls.

It's so cool being so high up. So beautiful and liberating. I feel so free. Who cares about sleazy men and stupid jobs?

The bus quits making awful noises, and sails through a flat section of road. My heart soars along with it. This must be how birds feel, I think as it gathers some speed, and—

Oh, my gosh. We're right on the mountaintop and the road ahead looks awful steep. Like, all I can see in front of us is clouds and blue sky. We're rushing toward a precipice. My stomach lurches and I get that sick, weightless feeling of being at the top of a rollercoaster before it begins its plunge into sheer hell.

I'm not good with heights. Seriously, I'm gonna need a sickbag.

*Crap.* What If I puke on this bus?

It'll be *soo* embarrassing. And gross. And the driver will probably kick me off.

The bus advances closer and closer to the edge.

Somebody starts squeaking like a terrified mouse.

*Oh, no,* it's me.

The bus stops.

"Come up front!" a voice booms.

*That* was not me. I lean out from my seat and crane my neck. Guess it was the driver. Unless it was some god, bellowing down from the heavens.

"E-excuse me?" I croak. My throat is all dried up.

"Come up here," he repeats, in a deep, rumbling voice. Kind of how a bear would sound if it could speak.

He shifts around in his seat and looks at me with a pair of bright green eyes.

I have no idea how I can tell they're green when I'm so far away. He also has a big, dark beard and his biceps are *epic*. Huge and rippling and covered in tattoos.

*Nothing* like a typical bus driver.

More like a scary mountain man who could eat me alive.

"You'll be more comfortable," he says in a softer tone.

I swallow hard. He's right. The front of a vehicle is

way more stable. If I'm gonna make it down this mountainside without totally humiliating myself, I need to give it my best shot.

"O-okay," I say and heave myself up.

The driver turns front again, but as I stagger down the bus on wobbly legs, I see him glance in his rearview mirror once or twice. I must look a sight. I burst out of the jewelry studio like a bat out of hell, and I was all hot and breathless by the time I got on the bus. And now I'm sure my face has gone deathly pale. Nothing I can do about that, though. I'll just sit down right here, opposite the driver's seat, and wait for this descent into hell to be over—

*Whoa.*

Up close, those eyes are ten times as intense. Like laser beams. They're pure emerald green, and the way he's looking at me... like he's trying to bore right into my soul, to dig up all my secrets. Shivers blast through me. This man is unearthly gorgeous.

My heart beats fast as I take in firm, lush lips, an angular jaw and cheekbones, and thick dark eyebrows and lashes. He's a fierce, scary wild man with the looks of a god.

Unfortunately, I'm so stunned by this hotness overload that I stumble backward.

The backs of my knees hit the edge of the seat and my ass drops down hard. I kind of bounce off the seat cushion and slither toward the ground. *Argh—*

At the last second, the driver's arm shoots out and he catches me.

His massive hand grips my belt buckle, holding me

in place. I look down at his equally massive forearm in awe. It's corded with muscle and covered with brightly colored tattoos. He draws me up into a standing position again. It can't be easy from this angle, but he makes it seem effortless.

"Steady." The ghost of a smile passes across his face, but all I can do is *stare*. He's the hottest bus driver on the planet. Scratch that. He's the hottest man I've ever seen in my life. His talents are seriously wasted driving a bus. He should have a starring role in *Game of Thrones* or something.

And he's still holding me by my belt. His knuckles are resting against the bare skin of my stomach. *Gulp.* Surely this shouldn't feel so good.

"Thanks," I manage to say.

"What's your name?"

"Jessica," I tell him.

"Nice to meet you, Jessica. I'm Ethan."

*Ethan. Hot name for a hot guy.*

He holds onto me for a moment longer. When he releases me, something like regret passes across his ridiculously handsome features. "Take a seat, right there." His voice is low, like he's trying not to scare me.

I'm too stunned to do anything other than obey him.

"Don't worry. It looks worse than it is," he says. "I'll drive real slow."

I look out of the windshield. For a moment, I'd forgotten all about the sheer drop in front of us. At least I can see the road from here. But it still looks pretty dang terrifying.

"You're not in any danger," he continues. "I'll never let anything bad happen to you."

That sounds nice, reassuring—

*Huh?* What does he mean, *never*?

I sense him looking at me and instinctively I turn my head back to him. *Wow.* There's something electrifying about his gaze. It sends sparks all through my body, making me feel hot and excitable.

I'm not used to having someone's attention on me like this. Sure, my ex used to stare at me a lot. Sometimes through binoculars. But this is different. This is not creepy at all. I feel like this hot stranger knows me. Like his soul is connecting with mine. And I know that makes no sense at all.

I swallow hard.

"Just relax." Ethan's voice is like a caress. He works the gearstick with his big, thick fingers and the bus starts moving.

2

*Jessica*

$O$kay, it's not so bad if I don't look out of the windshield. But I don't want Ethan to catch me staring at him, either. Instead, I focus my attention through the side window, watching as we hurtle below the tree line again.

"That's the worst of it over." His deep, rumbling voice cuts through the whining and rattling of the engine. I can tell he's trying to keep his tone soft for my benefit. He's sweet for a scary mountain man.

The road ahead of us starts to look more like a normal hilly road than a highway to hell. Thirty percent incline at most. Child's play.

"Whew. To think I was planning do this journey every day," I mutter.

Ethan gives a kind of jolt and his head whips toward

me. "You're not?"

"No. I…" I sigh. "Oh, it doesn't matter." I don't want to burden this kind, insanely hot stranger with my problems.

"What happened?" The urgency in his tone startles me. I swallow hard. He's mainly keeping his eyes on the road, but every time he glances at me, he has that fixated look. *Like he can't get enough of me?*

"Oh, I turned up to start my new apprenticeship today," I begin. "I was really looking forward to it. My boss is a big deal in his industry, and I was so happy that he'd chosen me out of a bunch of applicants. But, he—" I break off as another hot wave of humiliation crashes over me.

"He… what?" Ethan's voice is tense.

I take a big breath and let it out slowly. "He basically made it clear that he expects me to sleep with him."

"What!?" he bellows.

I jump. The sound is more like a beast's roar than something that could've come out of a human. But it's nothing compared to the anger burning in his eyes. He looks like he's ready to tear someone apart with his bare hands.

And… I like it. This might be really darn weird, but I don't feel scared. I feel like I want him to protect me.

"Yeah." I look down at my hands. "He made it seem like it was part of the job. Like, if I didn't sleep with him, I wouldn't get the apprenticeship."

"Where is he?" Ethan demands. His jaw is clenched so tight I can see the muscles bulging in his face.

"Uh…he's at the Jewelry Workshop in Brookville," I

blurt out, too stunned to wonder why he's asking.

He shakes his head angrily, muttering to himself. Maybe he's a psychopath, too, but his concern makes me feel safe. I get the feeling that if an axe-wielding maniac jumped on the bus right now, he'd do whatever it took to protect me. Hell, he'd probably knock them out with the force of that growly voice of his.

We pass through a bunch of switchbacks and he slows down even more, navigating each turn carefully. He's a good, careful driver, and I haven't gotten travel sick at all, I realize. I'm actually starting to enjoy this front-seat view of the mountains, sitting beside my personal super-sexy bus driver.

"You're running from something else."

My head snaps toward him. His eyes are burning brighter than ever. *How does he know that?*

"I sensed it," he says, without me asking.

I chew on my lower lip as I try to figure out what to tell him. The bus is going slower and slower. There must be a stop coming up. Disappointment pours through me. I like being alone in the bus with Ethan. I don't want some other passengers to come and intrude on our conversation.

The bus gives this almighty judder and stops altogether. I stare out of the window, confused. I don't see a stop, or anyone waiting by the roadside.

"Damn." Ethan jumps out of his seat and swings open the little door to his driving cabin.

*Holy crap.* Standing, he's even bigger than I realized. He's like a man mountain. A mountain of ripped, tattooed muscle.

"What is it?" I ask.

"The engine just quit." He jabs a button, the bus door opens with a hiss, and he jumps down the steps.

For no good reason, I follow him. A weird feeling is running through my body, all antsy, excitable, and I sense that the only thing that will fix it is being close to him.

He yanks on the hood and it opens with a loud, rusty-sounding creak. Clouds of steam are pouring out of engine, and there's an awful hissing sound.

"Uh-oh. It's not gonna blow, is it?"

Ethan looks at me like I'm the funniest thing ever. "Nope." His thick black eyebrows tug together as he peers at the engine.

Something is written across the front of it in another language. "Is that Russian?"

"Think so. This thing has to be at least fifty years old. It was probably brought over from the Soviet empire or some shit." He groans, sounding real pissed off. Then he sighs out something like sounds a lot like "Grandad."

"Huh?"

"This is my grandad's bus," he says. "I'm covering for him while he's out, having a hip operation."

"You're not a regular bus driver?"

"Hell, no." He shakes his head in distaste. "This piece of junk is ready for the wrecker's yard, and it usually runs three-quarters empty, but my grandad loves his job. If I didn't take over his shifts, the county would probably cancel the route and he'd be heartbroken."

Warmth floods my chest. He's not only incredibly

hot and uncannily perceptive, but he's got a kind heart as well. He's the dream man I never thought existed in real life.

"That's real nice of you," I say.

Those arresting eyes are fixed on me again. "Best decision I ever made."

My breath catches.

*Is he talking about me?*

That's a crazy thought. Where did it even come from?

But he's no longer looking pissed off. Instead, he looks kind of... hungry? His pupils are dilated, turning his eyes dark.

Dark and stormy, and fixated on me.

Shivers blast through me again, turning my nipples into aching peaks. I fold my arms to hide them, but luckily Ethan turns his attention back to the engine.

"This is not something I'm gonna be able to fix on the fly. Who knows if the spare parts even exist anymore—"

*Roooooarrr!* The grunt of a big engine cuts through the quiet. Purely on instinct, my gut tightens. Motorcycles, a whole bunch of them.

I watch as they roar past, looking anxiously for my ex-boyfriend's club colors. There are at least ten of them. Maybe there's some motorcycle convention in town. But I've got a bad feeling, worse than my day-to-day paranoia. Some spidey sense that my ex is close.

"What's wrong?" Ethan asks.

"Nothing." I'm already embarrassed that I burdened him with my apprenticeship calamity. I'm not about to tell him that this is the second time I've had issues with sleazy guys. "Anything I can do to help?" I say instead.

He crooks an eyebrow. "You happen to have a spare bus radiator, circa 1985, in your backpack?"

I giggle. "Darn. Knew I forgot something this morning."

"I'm sorry to tell you that this bus isn't going anywhere today." He clenches his jaw. "You have anyone who can come pick you up?" He spits the words out like a mouthful of dirt.

I sigh. "Usually I'd ask Ricky, but—"

"Ricky? He's your boyfriend?"

He looks all mad and… possessive? He hates the thought of me having a boyfriend. Is that because he *likes* me? My heart gives a big jolt.

"No, he's my brother," I manage to say. "But he's out of town on a job today. And I don't know anyone else." I look down the sloping mountain road dubiously. "Guess I could hitch a ride?"

"No!" he roars.

My head snaps toward him.

"It's not safe, Jessica. Promise me you'll never ever hitch a ride with a stranger." He looks so serious it scares me. But then he breaks into a smile, and it's like the sun coming out from behind a cloud. I get it. He's looking out for me. The thought twines around my heart.

"I promise," I say.

"Where do you live?"

"In Twin Falls."

He frowns thoughtfully. "There's a trail through the

forest, which starts fifty yards away. It will lead you right to Twin Falls. That's the best way for you to get home."

I stare into the densely-packed pine trees. "Really?" I've lived close to forests and areas of wilderness all my life, but I've never been one for hiking through them. I prefer to admire their intimidating beauty from a distance. "But is it safe?"

"Of course." He sounds surprised that I'm questioning it.

"Aren't there, like, bears and stuff?"

"Jessica, listen to me." His voice is a soft rumble.

Instinctively I turn, so I'm facing him.

"Nothing is going to hurt you in the forest." He lays one of his massive hands on his chest. "I promise you."

I blink, and... I believe him.

I stop questioning, and I just *trust* this big mountain man. Nothing is going to hurt me in the forest.

"You'd better get going. Before the weather changes." He looks up at the sky. It's still cornflower blue, but clouds are moving fast across it.

"Okay," I say, reluctantly. Because I don't want to walk away from Ethan. I want to stay right here with him. Listening to his voice. Drinking him in. I open my mouth to tell him I'll just hang out with him until the tow truck, or whatever, arrives. But that would be deeply weird. "Which way is the trail?" I ask instead.

"I'll show you."

He turns and leads me along the blacktop for a minute or so, then he points out a trail that disappears into the trees. It's narrow, not signposted.

I frown. "How did you know it was here?"

"I know these woods like the backs of my hands." He holds out one of those big, capable-looking hands. "Give me your phone."

My heart beats faster. He's going to tap his number into it.

*No, doofus.* He's opening my maps app.

"This is the route." His thick index finger traces the blue line that connects our current location to my tiny hometown. "You can follow it all the way, see?"

I nod. It looks straightforward, I note with a dash of relief.

"Okay, thanks so much, Ethan."

He gives me a long, smoldering look. I sense emotions warring behind those mesmerizing eyes of his, and I hold my breath.

"Enjoy the journey, Jessica," he says at last.

My shoulders slump. What did I expect anyway?

My heart is heavy as I turn away from him and plunge into the dark woods.

I'm not going to look back.

But with every step I take, loss tears through my soul. And it gets worse, the farther I go. It's a literal pain right in my center of my being.

Every bit of me is screaming for me to turn around again and *run* to him.

Throw myself into his big, sexy arms.

I only met him an hour ago, but suddenly, he feels like home.

## 3

*Ethan*

*I* watch as Jessica strides into the trees. My heart is beating so hard, I feel like it's going to leap right out of my chest.

She's mine.

I've found her at last.

Every fiber of my being aches to touch her, to take her in my arms. She's the most gorgeous thing I've ever laid eyes on.

Her long dark hair cascades down her back like a curtain of silk, and her ass is like two full, juicy peaches. I can't believe how beautiful and perfect she is. More lovely than I ever could've dreamed.

My beast is roaring for her, bellowing her name over and over, inflamed with lust.

All these years I've been alone, never believing there

was anyone out there for a solitary, forest dweller like me.

But here she is, arriving like a stroke of fate, when I least expected it.

When my grandad asked for my help on his bus route, I felt like the heavens were showering stars down on my head. Like the earth was tilting on its axis.

And now I know why.

My beast picked up her scent the moment she climbed on the bus and tapped her card on the reader. It's never been interested in women before. Sure, women sometimes flirt with me—especially when I'm driving the darn bus. But no one has ever awoken its mating urge. I thought I was destined to live out my days like a monk.

But by the time Jessica sat down on the backseat, it was telling me: she's *the one*.

I was so shocked, I almost crashed the dang bus. Thank goodness I was only going ten miles an hour.

And when I saw her up close for the first time... words can't describe the effect her beauty had on me. Love and arousal poured through me in a tidal wave.

When she passes through a bend in the track, I begin to follow her.

No way am I letting her walk through these woods alone. In fact, I'm never letting her out of my sight again. I'm going to keep her safe. Cherish and protect her, always.

I'm longing to run to her, tell her that she need never fear any danger again. She's mine, and I'll protect her with my last breath.

But I force myself to walk slowly, holding my beast back with everything I've got.

I don't want to scare her, make her think I'm a weirdo stalker.

She needs a gentle touch. I can tell she's been through a lot. I'm darn sure the jewelry designer asshole wasn't the first prick who's tried to force himself on her. She looked nervous when the motorcycles passed. There's something else in her past—or someone—that explains why her brother is the only person she can call when she's in a tight spot. I just know it, and fury pours through me at the thought. I vow I'll get hold of anyone who's ever hurt her and make them pay, three times over.

So, right now, I'm just going to make sure she gets home safe. I want her to feel secure with me. To understand I've only got her best interests at heart. And when I know where she lives, I'll go ask her out on a date like a regular human guy. She probably doesn't know about shifters. She'll need time to get used to the idea.

But I know she feels the connection between us, too. Her beautiful dark eyes kept running over me when she thought I wasn't looking, and I heard the hitch in her breathing, saw her pink little tongue running across her lips. And when she turned her back on me for what she thought was the last time—

My beast swells inside me.

I saw the naked regret in her eyes.

She's human. She probably understands nothing about how shifters; how we take our mates. But she senses it's wrong for us to be apart.

As the trail meanders, I make sure to stay just out of sight. If she turns around and sees me now, she'll probably call the cops. But staying so far away from her is killing me.

As is my cock. It's been like a rock ever since she walked down the bus and I touched her for the first time. Now it's so hard it hurts. I keep adjusting my pants over the bulge, fighting the urge to jerk off, take off some of the pressure.

When Jessica comes to a side trail, she pulls out her phone and checks the directions. Then she continues confidently along the main track. She's so smart. Doing so well for someone who said she doesn't like the forest much.

It made me sad when she said that, but I'll show her. Teach her that life in the forest is more real and beautiful than the artifices and bullshit of the outside world—

*Craaackk!* An almighty sound stops me in my tracks.

Thunder, rumbling in the distance.

*Darn.* I knew a storm was coming. I just hoped Jessica would make it back to Twin Falls before it arrived. High above the treetops, the sky has gotten dark and the scent of ozone is heavy in the air. Hopefully it'll hold off for another hour at least.

*Boom!* go the heavens, and a fork of lightning sears across the sky. Shit. There goes that idea.

She makes a small sound, of surprise or dismay, and it stabs me right in the heart.

Run to her, my beast urges. Snatch her up in your

arms, and lead her home to your cabin—where she belongs.

There's a long, tense silence, a feeling of the universe gathering itself. Then the rain starts to fall.

Fast, then stupid fast—a deluge, gushing from the sky like an upturned bucket.

She's gonna get soaked to the skin.

Time for plan B.

## 4

*Jessica*

*S*heesh, what is this—the apocalypse? Noah's Ark II?

The rain is falling in sheets. I duck beneath a pine tree, pressing myself against its trunk, but it doesn't make a whole lot of difference.

I feel like some angry gods just dunked an immortal-sized bucket of water over the world, and I am *drenched*. Shirt, jeans. Sneakers. My backpack is supposed to be waterproof, but I'm not about to check it and find out whether my notebooks and laptop have been annihilated.

I feel like even my underwear might be wet, and not in a good way.

Actually, truth be told, my panties *may* already have been a little damp before the flood started. But I didn't sign up for this kind of just-fell-into-the swimming-pool soaked.

And now I'm lost as well.

There I was, walking along, fantasizing...uh, thinking... about a certain unfeasibly sexy bus driver, and wishing I'd had the guts to give him my number, when the sky started gushing down on me. The pine trees don't keep the rain off much, but I thought I saw some kind of wooden shelter in the distance, so I jumped off the trail to go see. Unfortunately, it was a rotted old heap of wood, with no roof. *No problemo,* I thought. I'll just return to the trail. But my phone's GPS has stopped working, and I've gotten turned around, and... I have no idea which way leads back to the trail.

This is bad news.

I turn around and around in the dark wood and pouring rain, trying not to freak out.

*Think,* Jessica. What looks familiar?

Everything.

Nothing.

The tall pines all look the same. Freaking terrifying. They feel hostile, superior, like they're just hanging out, laughing at the little old humans who come and get lost in them.

Is it better to wait for my GPS to start working, or try to get back to the trail?

What if my phone's gotten too wet and it never starts working again? I swallow down a burst of panic.

The wind is picking up now, lashing the trees back and forth. It feels dangerous here.

I know I've got to stay calm, but my heart's beating hard and I'm kinda hyperventilating—

Okay. I can do this. If I keep the shelter behind me, I just need to head away from it. I start picking my way through the undergrowth, back to where I hope the trail is. But the howling wind is scaring the bejeezus out of me. I go faster and faster, twigs whipping across my face, creepers catching at my ankles. I think that's the trail, ten feet ahead. I can just make out a stretch of bare earth.

*Creeeakkk...!* What is that? There's a rushing sensation overhead. I look up, and—

"Oh, my god!" I let out a wild scream as a massive, dark shape hurtles right at me. A falling tree! My heart leaps into my throat. There's no time to move. All I can do is squeeze my eyes shut, waiting for the end to come.

*Bumpphh.* Something hits me from the side. And then I'm flying through the air. All the breath whooshes out of me, and I hit the ground. But not hard. There's an earsplitting crash right beside me, and the earth shakes.

My eyes flutter open.

*What happened? Am I dead?*

The rain is still falling; the pine trees are still towering overhead. But I'm lying someplace real comfy, and... *Ethan?*

Either I'm unconscious and having some real trippy dream, or my stupidly sexy bus driver is staring down at me, his features drawn with concern.

"You're safe now," he says in that delicious rumbling voice of his.

"Am I still alive?" I croak out.

A smile tugs at the corners of his lips. "Very much so."

"A tree—"

"Just came down over there."

I turn my head where he's indicating and, *argh*. There it is, all massive and horizontal, smaller trees flattened all around it. "It almost hit me. I thought—" I choke back a sob.

"It's okay, I got to you in time."

"You saved me."

He shrugs like it was nothing.

"I was lost," I blurt out. "I couldn't figure out how to get back to the trail. And then the tree—" My voice turns high and tight, betraying the fear I've been trying to tamp down.

"Shush, I've got you." His voice is soothing, and I realize he's *literally* got me. The reason why I feel so luxuriously comfortable right now is because his arms are around me, protecting me from the forest floor.

I have an urge to press my face to his big muscly chest and sob in relief.

Wow, that would be embarrassing.

"Does anything hurt?" He looks worried.

"Uh, I dunno." I shake out my limbs one at a time. "So far, so good."

"Let's get you up." He lifts up from me, and I shiver as my man-sized heating pad disappears. He springs to his feet and reaches for me. I only met him a couple of hours ago, but somehow it doesn't feel that way, as I cling to him.

He makes sure I'm safely on my feet again, then he scans me up and down, his eyebrows furrowed. "Are you okay? Any scrapes or bruises?"

I examine my arms. Miraculously, there's not a mark on me. "Don't think so. Still in one piece, I think."

"Good." He looks relieved. "We should get going. I think the storm's gonna get worse."

"Uh, sure." I look around wildly. "Where's the trail?"

"Over there." He points in the opposite direction from the fallen tree.

"Great." I roll my eyes. "Looks like I was even walking in the wrong direction when I almost got taken out by the tree-pocalypse."

His frown deepens, then he breaks into a smile. "You have a great sense of humor, you know?"

"Gotta look on the bright side," I mumble, but I'm secretly pleased by the compliment. It drives my brother crazy how I'm constantly joking about serious things.

Something passes across Ethan's eyes—something tender but heated at the same time. He insists on carrying my backpack, then he takes my hand and starts to lead me through the sodden woods.

Yes—*he takes my hand.* His big thick fingers envelope my much smaller ones. Despite the deluge, his palms are warm and dry and comforting, and...

It's like an electric current is running between us. Does he feel it, too? For a moment, I can't breathe for the tingles spilling through my body.

All I can do is stumble after him.

IN A FEW MINUTES, we're back on the trail. It's a sea of mud now, channels of water running down either side.

Ethan pauses under the shelter of a monster pine tree. "Wish I had a waterproof shirt I could give you." He indicates his tank top with a wry smile.

It's completely soaked and clinging to his incredibly buff torso like a second skin, outlining every rippling muscle. He's as wet as I am, but somehow he looks hotter than ever. His hair has come out of its man bun and it hangs loose around his shoulders. He's a sexy wild man; like some awesome god of the storm. Heat pours through me. I might still be recovering from my near-death experience, but I've never felt more alive. Just the sight of him is doing all kinds of things to my body.

"Oh, you've done enough, trust me," I say. Then I frown as my brain finally catches up. "But how did you find me here?"

"I followed you. I wanted to make sure you got home safe," he says, as though it's obvious.

I stare at him. If these were the words of a stalker, I'd run screaming into the wilderness right now, deadly thunderstorm be damned. But somehow I know they're not. I can't explain it, I just know, deep in my soul, that I can trust him. I understand he'd never hurt me.

"Thank you," I say instead.

"It's my pleasure, believe me." He gives me another

one of those long, intense looks, like he can hardly tear his eyes away from me. *Like he's falling for me.* My heart beats fast. That can't be right, can it? We only just met.

But... I also feel this crazy *connection* between us. It's like we complete each other, or something. Like he's a part of me that's been missing all my life, and now that I've found him, I'm finally whole. I've never felt that way before. Heck, I didn't even know it was possible to feel that way.

Gooseflesh breaks out on my arms, and I rub at them.

Ethan's eyes darken with concern. "Let's get you inside," he says.

"But where?" I scan the densely packed trees in both directions. If there's a cave nearby, I definitely don't see it.

"I'm taking you back to my cabin. It's a half-mile away."

"You live in the forest?"

"We'll be safe there." As if he can sense my hesitation, he says in a softer tone, "I'd never do anything you're not comfortable with. I just want to take care of you, Jessica."

I blink. *Take care of me.* He's the opposite of every other guy I've met in my life. They've all wanted to take things *from* me. I've spent the last year on high alert, always ready for my ex's googly eyes to appear, for him to make good on his threats and manipulation. But Ethan... He's come looking for me in the middle of a storm, abandoning his grandad's broken-down bus in the process, then saved me from being squished by a tree...

Now he's taking me to his cabin.

Maybe it's dumb to trust a complete stranger. But Ethan is not a stranger, and I've never felt so sure of anything in my life.

"Okay, let's go," I say.

He keeps a tight grip on my hand as he draws me along, dodging the worst of the mud. The wind and driving rain snatch my breath away and I'm starting to shiver like crazy, but I know that as long as I keep hold of Ethan's hand, I'll be safe. I can see how well he knows the forest, how he exists at one with it. All I need to focus on is getting indoors—

We pass through a bend in the trail.

"Oh shit," Ethan mutters, at the same moment that a loud rushing sound rises above the howling wind and thrashing trees.

I step out from behind him and literally feel my eyes bulge when I see what he's looking at.

## 5

*Ethan*

*T*he little river which usually meanders through the forest, and doesn't do a whole lot more than wet my calves, has turned into a raging torrent. It's fast and angry-looking, with broken-off branches caught up in its flow.

Kinda awesome. At least, if I was alone right now, I'd think so. I'd stand and watch it for a while. Maybe take a daredevil swim. But right now, I've got Jessica to take care of. And I don't want her to experience a moment of fear or uncertainty.

I turn to her. Her dark hair is plastered to her face and her skin is paler than before. She looks like a wild, gorgeous creature of the storm. But she's scared. And that's the last thing I want.

"How are we going to cross it?" she murmurs.

"It's nothing," I tell her. "I cross it every day."

"Like this?" Her lovely arched eyebrows tug together.

"Well, it's usually a little calmer." I laugh.

She bites her lip and suddenly, she looks so vulnerable, my heart aches. Without another thought, I put my arms around her and sweep her up into my embrace.

She gasps in surprise, but then her slender arms lift up and loop around my neck, naturally, like she's done it a hundred times before. My heart leaps. Because she's *mine*. Everything happens so naturally between us because we're supposed to be together.

*Damn.* And the feeling of her in my arms. I bite back a groan of desire. Her luscious body fits so perfectly against mine. Her perfect round tits rise and fall in time with her breathing, and her beautiful face is only inches away. I take in the deep, sparkling amber of her irises, make out every long, dark lash. Her full rose-pink lips are so temptingly close. I'd only have to dip my head and I'd be claiming them with my own. My dick gets even harder at the thought.

I'd do anything for the chance to kiss her. Risk anything; endure any suffering.

*But it's not gonna happen until she shows me she wants me,* I tell my beast, pushing back on its feral desire.

When I take a step closer to the bank, she whimpers. An answering jab of pain goes through my heart. Doesn't she know I'd never let anything bad happen to her?

"Just relax, honeybun, we'll be across in a second," I say. I step carefully down the steep bank and wade into the water. The rocks underfoot are slippery, and the loose branches slam into my knees, but my tread is sure. I take another step, and another one. The water charges past my thighs. It's freezing cold, but I barely feel it, because the warmth of my mate's body radiates right through me.

The feeling of her fingers clinging to the back of my neck is a bliss I never could have imagined. With every breath, I inhale her scent. The rain has diluted it, but it's still there, sweet and heady and intoxicating.

My bear rumbles with pleasure as we make our way through the river. It's in no hurry now, wanting to savor this moment for as long as possible.

I'm trying to focus on getting her home, and not imagine how incredible she'll feel when there are no clothes between us, no storm hammering me on all sides. But it's no use. My cock is surging like a heat-seeking missile. I'm desperate to claim her sweet body, to make her mine forever.

Three more strides and I'll be at the opposite bank—

*Clunk!* Something smashes into the back of my thigh, almost taking me down. I stagger and bite back a curse.

"Ethan!" Jessica screams.

"Sorry." I make my voice soft and soothing. "It's okay."

"No, you're hurt." Her eyes widen in concern.

There's a twinge in my chest. I'm not used to folks being concerned for me. "I'm fine," I grunt. But if I'm honest, I like the feel of it. Her worrying for me.

The offending item zips past. Half a darn tree trunk.

I grind my teeth together. I should've been watching for shit like that. *Be more careful, doofus. You're transporting the most precious thing in the world.*

Finally, we're at the far bank. I hold Jessica more tightly as I clamber up the slippery slope.

When I'm back on solid ground again, my heart lifts. There are no more obstacles in my way. I'm taking Jessica back to my cabin.

And that means she's mine. My bear is bounding in joy beneath my chest. I long to shift, throw her on my back, and run home, as fast as my four paws can carry me.

She's not ready for that yet, though. First I need to show her the man I am. And not scare the hell out of her in the process.

But it's going to be hard. Because I'm already enthralled with her. My obsession is taking hold. I'm desperate to be closer to her, to explore her without any constraints. The physical attraction is too strong to deny. But it's more than that—I can't wait to find out all about her. What makes her happy, excited. What her dreams are, and how I can help her fulfill them.

I peer down at her. Her lips are parted and she looks a little stunned. "Are you okay?"

She breaks into a smile and my heart jolts in response.

"Never better," she says.

She's being ironic, of course. But I love how she's so tough, so spirited. The perfect mate for a bear. *For me.*

"I'll protect you from anything," I tell her. "You don't

have to worry about anything ever again. You'll be safe and cared for, always."

Her eyes widen in surprise. It's a lot to hear, I know that. But I need her to understand how much she means to me.

"That sounds… nice," she says haltingly.

I stop breathing.

*She's never felt like that before.*

The thought hits me like a viper's strike: *she's never felt safe.* I'm desperate to ask her what she's been running from, but there'll be time for all that later. Now, I need to focus on getting her out of the storm.

"Almost there," I tell her, picking up my pace.

With every step, my beast swells inside me.

Soon, she'll be in my lair. The rest of the world shut out. Just me and Jessica, and this one night to make her mine.

## 6

*Jessica*

When we're safely across the river, I expect Ethan to set me down on my feet again. But he doesn't. He keeps right on, striding through the downpour with me in his arms.

"Aren't I getting kinda heavy?" I shout above a vicious gust of wind.

His burning gaze locks onto mine. "Nope. You're as light as a feather."

Okay, then. I guess I could get used to this—being carried in the strong embrace of a mountain man. My head is resting in the crook of his neck, and I'm fighting the impulse to snuggle into him. His deep, spicy masculine scent is filling my nostrils, while his wet hair falls over my face, protecting me from the worst of the rain.

We're also going a lot faster now. Instead of walking

at my stumbling pace, he's hurtling along like he's got a homing device attached to him.

Before long, a log cabin emerges from between the trees. It's rustic but cozy-looking, with curtains up at its two square windows and a shiny red front door.

This is it. This is where I enter his lair. Shivers of anticipation race through me.

I guess I should be a little apprehensive at least. But, to be honest, all I can think about is how much I want to be alone with him.

And I guess I'll be staying here all night long, because the rain isn't showing any signs of letting up. Okay, this part is a little scary, not least because I've never done more than kiss a man before.

In fact, the rain seems to be falling faster than ever as Ethan charges to the front door. He shoulders it open, no key required. Guess there's no one to break into a place this remote. Or, maybe it's more that nobody would dare.

And we're in. He kicks the door shut, and… silence. At last.

My ears ring from the sudden quiet. The only sound is water sploshing on the wooden floor at it drips off us.

"Wow, it's so good when it stops," I say.

"Kinda brutal, wasn't it?" He grins at me. I have the feeling that he's not a guy who usually smiles a lot, and I'm happy if I have this effect on him.

And he's still not putting me down.

Ethan seems to be content to keep right on, cradling me in his arms. I feel his massive chest rising and falling, hear his breath going in and out. It has a weird rumbly kind of sound, but I like it. It feels like home, somehow.

As he gives me that intense, fixated look of his again, I realize how I must look. Take how I looked on the bus and multiply by ten. Hair all plastered down, red nose, mascara probably smudged panda-style under my eyes.

I swipe at my face, trying to dry it with my wet hands. "Gosh, I'm like a drowned rat."

He frowns. "Jessica, don't ever say things like that about yourself. You're beautiful. A beautiful, strong woman."

My mouth falls open. Not *too darn cheerful*; not always getting myself into scrapes, but *strong*. I glow inside. I love the way Ethan makes me feel about myself.

He moves in closer. Those gorgeous, firm lips swim in front of my vision. *He's going to kiss me.* My eyelids fall shut and my lips purse, ready to receive his kiss, and—

His breath catches, like he just remembered something.

"I'm so sorry. You must be freezing." He lowers me to the ground and sets me gently on my feet. "I shouldn't have let you stand here, cold and wet."

"It's okay," I mumble, trying to keep the disappointment out of my voice.

"It's not." He shakes his head quickly like he's mad at himself. Darn, that's the last thing I want after all he's done for me.

"Maybe I could get a shower?" I suggest.

"Yes." He brightens. "Let me show you where the bathroom is."

Trying not to feel too much like a deflating balloon, I follow him through the cabin, my wet socks squelching with every step.

I take in a cozy, rustic, living space, with well-loved furniture scattered around. But in the corner, two plasma screens glow above a professional-looking keyboard. It seems so out of place, so not a part of this rugged mountain man's world that I stop and gawk at it.

Ethan turns back, with a questioning look. "It's just work," he says dismissively.

"What work do you do?"

"I'm an app designer."

My mouth falls open. I'd assumed he chopped down trees or wrestled alligators or something. "That's so cool."

He shrugs. "It pays the bills."

"There's a lot of layers to you, Ethan."

"What do you mean?"

"Oh, good Samaritan. Fearless forest dweller. Famous app designer."

He grins good naturedly. "Not exactly true, but I'm happy if you see me that way."

And definitely some layers I wouldn't mind unpeeling, I think, as my eyes zone in on his wet tank top again.

At the rear, there's a hallway, and a whole other section of the cabin. This place is deceptively huge, like it's had an extension built on the back of it.

"Bedrooms." Ethan indicates several doors going off the hallway. "And bathroom."

That's a whole lot of space for one mountain man, I muse. It's more like a family home.

The bathroom is simple, but it has good-quality white units, and it smells of cleaning products. He shows me how to adjust the temperature on the shower, then he hands me a couple of towels, which smell freshly laundered.

A mountain man who cares about laundry? For some reason, that's ridiculously sexy. Just when I thought Ethan couldn't be any more intriguing.

"You got a change of clothes in your backpack?" he asks.

"Nope," I say cheerfully. "And if I did, I think they'd be as wet as the ones I'm wearing." It's already occurred to me that I don't have a single dry thing to change into, but after everything I've been through today, that's small beans.

"I'll see if I can figure something out." He backs out of the bathroom, dipping his head like he's embarrassed or something.

I glance at my reflection in the mirror. My mascara has indeed smudged. Although, it's not as comical as I expected. It's more like smudged liner.

*You're beautiful,* he said. Even when I looked like this.

I repeat his words in my head, warmth pouring through me. He likes me. He's into me. Which feels exciting, but hella nerve-wracking at the same time.

I peel my clothes off, laughing to myself at just how drenched they are. When I wring them out in the sink, a bucketload of water comes out.

Then I turn on the shower and adjust the temperature just like Ethan showed me.

The hot water feels *incredible*. "Oh, my god," I whisper. I let it cascade over me until I'm warmed all the way through, then I reach for some shower gel. It's an eco-brand, and it's scented with sandalwood and bergamot. *That's* the smell I was picking up while Ethan was marching me through the forest. A dart of yearning goes through me as I remember the sensation of being in his arms. So close to him. Surrounded by his strength and his wild masculinity.

I shake myself. *Okay, quit fantasizing and focus on getting clean. You're not the only one who needs a hot shower here.*

When I'm done, I dry off fast, then I wrap the towel around myself. I open the bathroom door a crack, and hesitate.

That thing I was saying about small beans? Not true.

My cheeks warm as I absorb the fact I'm about to exit the bathroom wearing just a towel, in front of the hottest man in the universe. He's gonna know I'm naked underneath it. I'll be *so* exposed.

And the worst part is—the thought of that turns me on like crazy.

"Jessica?" Ethan's voice comes from somewhere deep in the cabin. I close my eyes, letting it roll through me. I love the way my name sounds in his mouth.

"Yeah?" I reply.

"I put something out for you on the shelf. It might fit you."

Shelf... shelf. *There*, farther down the hallway. I grab

a pile of fabric. There's a white T-shirt and a pair of patterned pink shorts. Still with the tags on. But who did he buy them for? Deciding I'll worry about that later, I retreat into the bathroom and pull them on.

They fit. They actually look pretty cute. The kind of things I might've chosen for myself. Then I flip on the light above the mirror and look a little closer. *Annnd* I can just make out my nipples beneath the fabric, poking up like little pebbles. Shoot. He's going to see them. If I don't keep my arms folded the whole time. And as for the fact I'm not wearing panties…

Gulp.

This is a whole lot better than wearing a towel, but I still feel so naked. I'd better make sure I sit with my legs together. And don't get wet again. Anywhere.

I can do this.

Taking a deep breath, I creep out of the bathroom.

Right away, the last part of my plan fails.

## 7

*Jessica*

*B*ecause Ethan's standing in the middle of the living room in a fresh white tank top and blue jeans. His hair is pulled up in a man bun again, and he looks hotter than ever. Heat flares between my thighs, and I swear my knees go weak.

"You got dry?" I say confusedly.

He thumbs over his shoulder. "I took a shower out the back. I've got an outdoor shower rigged up."

"You showered in the storm?"

"Wasn't gonna get any wetter." He grins. "I wanted to make sure I was here when you came out."

My heart flutters and I fall for him a little more. He's too awesome to be real. So strong and masculine, but so considerate as well. Like some crazy fantasy I dreamed up.

His gaze flickers to my new outfit and away again, like he's dying to stare at me, but he's trying not to be obvious about it.

"Hope I'm not stealing someone else's clothes?" I blurt out, as the green-eyed monster rises up in me. I swear I've never felt like this before. So *possessive* and territorial.

He looks thoughtful. "No, I bought them last week when I was out shopping in Twin Falls." He shrugs. "Wasn't sure why at the time. Look like they were made for you, though."

"Oh," I say, and there's a weird little lurch in my chest. Is he saying he bought them because he somehow *knew* he was going to meet me? The hairs on my forearms stand up. Everything that's happened between us so far feels like it's been stage-managed by something bigger than the two of us. What a crazy, exciting thought.

"Here," he hands me a steaming mug of tea, and gestures at his brown leather sofa. "Take a seat."

The sofa is as comfy as it looks and I sink into it gratefully. There's a fireplace on the opposite side of the room, and a bunch of logs are crackling and popping in a soft orange glow. I can see all the care Ethan has taken to make his place into a real home.

"Feeling better?" he asks.

"So much." I sip the tea. "Wow, this is amazing."

"It's herbal. Some stuff I grew out back," he says carelessly.

*And* he makes his own tea. And makes out like that's nothing.

"Are you hungry? Got some stew heating up."

Right on cue, my belly rumbles like a beast. *Oof.* Not very sexy or ladylike. "Sorry," I squeak. "I haven't eaten for a while. Since breakfast actually."

His eyes turn tender again. "That's no good. You need to keep your strength up."

He goes to the kitchen and stirs at something on the stove. Meanwhile, I grab my backpack and open it gingerly. By some miracle, my laptop is still dry inside its waterproof sleeve, and my phone still works. I've sure tested the manufacturers' claims to the max today.

I swipe on my phone screen. My brother will be wondering where the hell I am. And probably freaking out. I stare into space, trying to figure out how to communicate to him that I'm fine right now. I can't exactly tell him that I'm staying in the cabin of a big muscly mountain man. He'll probably call the FBI or mountain rescue, or something.

*Darn.* I hate lying to him, but sometimes it's the only way to keep Ricky's twitchy psyche under control. At last, I type out:

*Hey, Ricky. Some storm huh? Did you get home ok? Luckily I avoided the worst of it, and I'm gonna stay in Brookville tonight.*

Not *exactly* a lie.

I hit send.

But I get a fail signal. I try again and again, but nada.

"Everything okay?" Ethan is carrying two steaming plates of food.

"Yeah, just my brother. I need to tell him I'm safe."

He frowns. "He'll be worrying about you. That's not

good. But I don't think there'll be any signal until the storm is over."

I sigh. "Not much I can do, then. Hopefully he'll figure that I took shelter someplace."

Trying my best to sit in a way that keeps my legs together and shirt hanging loose over my boobs, I dig in.

It's beef stew and it tastes real good. I tell him so.

"Not a lot of restaurants around here, so I had to make sure I could cook my own food," he says in that careless way of his. Like his talents are not a big deal.

"Do you like living out in the wilderness?" I ask. I'm burning with curiosity about his mountain-man life-style, but trying my best to act casual.

"Yeah. I love the peace. And I've got a few family members living in cabins around here, if I'm in the mood for some company." There's a sparkle in his eye, as if he knows I'm really trying to ask whether he's a complete recluse.

"And you don't miss the city?"

He looks appalled. "Reckon my soul would shrivel up if I had to live surrounded by all that concrete."

He has a point, I think, gazing around the cabin. He's got everything he needs right here. Out of nowhere, an image pops into my mind of me sitting at the kitchen table, designing jewelry, while he's designing his apps at the computer. It would be so cozy—

I startle. Where did *that* thought come from?

We both eat fast. When we're done, I jump up and insist on washing the dishes. His kitchen is just perfect, too. Small, but well-equipped. Through the window above the sink, I can see the storm raging. It eased off a little while we were eating, but now it's gathering force again.

When I turn back to the living area, a crack of thunder rips right overhead.

"Sounds like it's gonna take the roof off," I say with a nervous laugh.

Ethan reaches behind himself and knocks on one of the wooden walls. "Don't worry, this place is solid. Even a twister couldn't take it out. That's how my grandad built it."

"The same one whose bus you're now driving?"

"Yup. See how I owe him one?"

Then the smile drops from his face. "Jessica, you're safe here. You know that?"

I go still. I do know that. I only met Ethan today, but I feel like I've known him for a lifetime. Maybe many lifetimes. "Yes," I say in a quiet voice.

"Come sit down." He taps on the seat beside him. His eyes burn into me and I shiver. I'm powerless to do anything other than obey him. If he's trying to hypnotize me, I'm all in. This gorgeous mountain man has me under his spell.

I walk over and perch on the edge of the cushion beside him. Tingles run through me, quickly turning into a deep throb between my thighs. I swallow hard.

I'm longing for him to take me into his arms, throw me down on the sofa and kiss me senseless. I think he feels the same. But what if I've got it all wrong? I'm not good with guys. Not good with guys who aren't sleazy assholes, anyway.

"Tell me what happened," he says.

I blink. "When?"

"What were you running from, Jessica?" His voice is serious and I sense that every bit of his attention is focused on me.

*How does he know?* I wonder. But I already know the answer to that: he just does. He reads me.

I take a big in-out breath. "My ex—well, a guy I was dating—"

A snarl breaks from his throat. "You had a boyfriend?"

I startle. "Y-yeah, but it wasn't serious. To me anyway. We'd only been on a few dates, and I wasn't sure about him." I clasp my hands together. He has that look in his eyes again—the one he had on the bus. Like he's already planning to hunt down my ex and take him out.

And I have no idea why that's making my clit throb out of control.

I clear my throat. "But he got weird. Stalkery. When I told him I didn't want to see him anymore, he threatened to kill me. So, Ricky and I had to move towns. I've basically been hiding out ever since. Wondering when he's going to catch up with me."

Ethan is working his jaw and clenching his fists, looking like he's about ready to burst out of his skin.

"He's a biker?"

I frown. "Yeah, how did you—?"

"I saw you were afraid of the bikes today."

"Oh." I bite my lip. "Yeah. He's a member of a bunch of assholes, also known as Bigwood Brotherhood MC. I think I saw their dumb colors." I roll my eyes. "Apparently they're on the lookout for me, too."

He takes my hand. "You've been scared for a long time."

I nod.

"But you make light of it."

I shrug. "What can I do? Ricky wants me to stay at home indefinitely, hide myself away from the world. But I'm not like that."

A ghost of a smile passes across his handsome face. "Of course, you're not. You're so full of life. So gutsy."

My heart gives a little jump. But then Ricky's words rise up from the depths. "Some would say naïve," I mutter.

Ethan frowns. "None of this is your fault, Jessica. You hear me? You're beautiful and good-hearted, and some men prey on that. But don't change for other people. Including your brother—even if he means well. Don't let the world take away your shine."

I stare at him wordlessly. Somehow, I feel like there's more of me when I'm with Ethan. Like I bloom under his praise.

"And you don't need to worry about these bikers anymore." He strokes my palm with his callused thumb. "I'll take care of them."

He's offering to deal with an entire MC? If it was anyone else, I'd think they were crazy. But I feel that he's stronger than all of them put together. There's something superhuman about him, something that my subconscious is registering, but I don't have a word for.

"What are you—?" I begin, with no idea how I'm going to end that sentence.

Resolution gathers in his eyes. "I'm a shifter. You know what that is?"

I shake my head.

He lifts my hand and presses it to his chest. "Feel this?"

I feel the heat of his body scorching my hand; the strong, steady pump of his heart. And something else—a rumbling, vibrating sensation that matches his exhalations.

I gaze at him in wonder.

"I have a bear inside me," he says.

"A bear," I repeat. I stare at him in silence for a few beats. Maybe it's crazy, but the word feels so right on my lips. Like, of course he does. I think I knew deep down, from the moment I laid eyes on Ethan, that this huge, muscleman could not just be a regular human.

"S-so, you shift between your bear and human sides?" I stutter.

He gives a solemn nod. "Does that freak you out?"

I shake my head slowly. "No."

"How does it make you feel?" He's looking at me so intensely, like he's hanging on my next word. I feel all breathless and overwhelmed.

"Curious," I say. *Man*, that's an understatement. But I don't know how he'd react if I told him the truth:

Wet. Turned on like crazy at the thought that my mountain man crush is half-man and half-beast. I press my thighs together to quell the ache in my pussy.

"You want to know what shifters are like?"

I nod eagerly.

He moves a little closer, until he's looming over me. "We're loyal.

Protective as hell.

We'd fight to the death for our mates.

We mate for life.

We have lots of cubs."

I can't drag my eyes away from him. Every sentence lights a charge inside me.

"How does that sound?"

My heart beats fast. Something tells me doesn't mean in general. He's asking how it sounds to me, specifically.

"I know it's a lot to hear," he continues. "But you've got to know what a shifter is like. How obsessive and possessive we are when we take our mate."

*Holy crap.*

His eyes are full of fire, and I'm trembling like crazy. Already, I'm imagining myself pregnant with Ethan's cubs. It's a scary, exciting thought. Especially since I'm still a virgin.

I sense that now is not the time for subtlety. "It sounds like everything I ever wanted," I manage to say.

He lets out a sigh of pure need and it's a sexy, sexy sound. Then his gaze fixates on my lips. "I want to kiss you," he growls.

*Oh, god.* My heart is almost beating out of my chest. I'm ridiculously inexperienced. And I have no idea what it's going to be like to kiss a shape-shifter. All I know is that I want Ethan to kiss me more than I've wanted anything in my life.

I nod. "Uh huh. I mean, yes, please kiss me."

He wraps his big arms around me, comes in close and *possesses* my mouth.

It's like no kiss I've had before.

It's fierce, hungry. Blissful. His lips are so firm and masculine, but so soft and lush at the same time.

He draws me against his huge body, and I wrap my arms around him, too. I feel so protected, so safe… so aroused by him. When his hands go around my back and slide under my T-shirt, a little moan spills out of me.

He draws back and looks at me seriously. "Is this okay? I don't want to rush you, Jessica."

I bite my lip. "I've never done this before, but I am so ready for you, Ethan."

His breath catches. "Never?"

"Never." I give a nervous laugh. "I never wanted to, like, get naked with a guy before."

He lays his hands around my waist. They're so big, they almost encircle it. "No one's ever seen this body before?"

I shake my head. "Nope."

"Touched it?"

"No." I laugh.

He lets off a growl, and I see it—see his bear surfacing, its features changing his face. It's scary, but kind of awesome.

His mouth crashes against mine, and when he angles his jaw and plunges his tongue in, I open for him. Oh, it feels so good, dancing around mine, exploring my mouth. I cling to him, my whole body throbbing with need. My nipples are so hard they hurt, while I'm pretty sure I've soaked these little shorts right through.

When Ethan draws back and raises the hem of my shirt, I go still.

"Can I see them?" he says.

I nod. I'm a little nervous, but so ready for him. And everything feels so right. The storm is battering the windows, but the fire is crackling in the hearth, and I'm safe indoors, protected by this big, sexy shifter.

I bite my lip as he lifts up my shirt and bares my breasts for the very first time. I see them in my peripheral vision, exposed to his burning gaze.

"So beautiful, honeybun, so perfect," he growls. He pulls my shirt right over my head, then he cups my tits in his huge hands. I remember how sexy his hands looked this morning, working the gearstick. And now here they are exploring my bare body. And his touch is incredible. He squeezes my tits gently, then he dips his head and takes one of my nipples into his mouth.

*Holy hell.* This is something else. He sucks on one, and then the other, impatiently, like he can't get enough. Waves of bliss pour through me, and my pussy spasms, hungry for his touch. I grind it against him to relieve the pressure.

Against something rock-hard and unyielding. I glance down. Oh, it's his cock, huge and straining beneath his jeans, like it's trying to escape.

Like it wants to get to me.

I've never seen a cock before. I've never been that interested in them. I was actually starting to wonder if I was frigid. But suddenly there's nothing I want more in the world than to see Ethan naked. I take hold of his shirt and yank it up.

He draws back from my tits, a wicked look in his eye. "You want my clothes off?" he demands.

"I want to see all of you," I say.

He tugs his shirt over his head and casts it aside. I drink in the sight of his huge, muscular torso. Then I let my hands loose, running all over the contours and ripples. It's incredible, velvety, hard. Stupidly arousing. I explore his abs, then those sexy diagonal grooves of muscle. When I reach his belt buckle, I hesitate.

I have no idea what I'm doing. He's going to think I'm so inexperienced.

He grabs his cock through his jeans. "You want this?"

I nod. "I want it bad." I don't know where these words are coming from, but I'm not gonna hold back. This is happening.

"You want it inside you?"

"Yeah," I say, although now I can see the outline of it in his hand, I'm starting to appreciate just how big it is.

A look of understanding passes across his face. "No rush, honeybun. I'm gonna wait until you're good and ready for me. Until having me inside you is about all you can think about."

*Damn*, it's pretty much all I can think about right now.

He takes my hand and presses it against the bulge. It's like a beer can or something. One of those real tall ones. There's no way in a million years this is gonna fit inside me.

"We'll go slow," he murmurs in my ear, and

somehow this powerful guy telling me he's gonna be gentle with me is the sexiest thing I can imagine.

"Now, let me see you." He lays me back on the couch, then he reaches for the waistband of my shorts and pulls them down. *Oh, god.* I swallow hard.

A sound of pure need escapes his throat. "You're wet, huh?"

"A little." Understatement of the century.

He tugs my shorts all the way off, then he scrunches them in his hand and presses them to his face. "You smell so good," he growls. "That beautiful virgin scent."

*Ohh.* My cheeks heat. Embarrassing, but as hot as hell.

Then he shoves my legs apart.

I give a squeak of surprise. I was just getting used to the fact that I was naked. And now I'm all spread open for him.

"Beautiful," he purrs. He spreads my lips with two fingers, examining me. I clap a hand over my mouth, squirming under his scrutiny.

"So pink and perfect," he growls. "Such a pretty little hole. No one's ever seen it before?"

"No, you're definitely the first," I mumble through my fingers.

He makes a sound of satisfaction, then he slides a thick finger into me. It feels good, but he doesn't get very far. "You've never had anything inside you?"

I shake my head.

"No vibrator? Nothing?"

"No." I never wanted to experiment. I was waiting for Ethan to be my first. I get that now.

He makes a deep sound of satisfaction. "Let me taste this little pussy."

Before I know what's happening, his head is between my thighs and his tongue is lapping at my slit. I'm so wet, so sensitive; it's almost too much to take. He seems to sense it, licking me everywhere but my aching clit. Teasing me with light strokes. Plunging his tongue inside me, like he's trying to see how deep it can go.

When he finally moves onto my clit, I'm ready for him. I tangle my fingers in his hair and hold him close.

"Oh, god," I gasp as his tongue works up this incredible rhythm. I'm grinding my hips against his face, all kinds of sounds coming from my mouth. I probably sound feral, but I don't care. All I can think about is my sexy man pleasuring me with his amazing tongue.

Inside me a kind of trembling, shuddering sensation is building. It's getting stronger and stronger, and...

I go off.

I explode,

Right in his face. I scream and cry out his name as waves of bliss pour through me.

He keeps right on going, playing me like a musical instrument, until I'm all orgasmed out.

"That's what all the fuss is about," I whisper, weak and breathless.

He lifts up and arches over me. "First time?"

I nod. "First time."

A look of gratification passes across his face. "You better get used to it, honeybun, because you're gonna come every day from now on. With my tongue, my fingers, and my cock. Especially my cock." He holds me close and kisses me deeply again. "When you're ready for it."

I just had a colossal orgasm, yet Ethan's kiss is making me hungry for more.

"Oh, I'm ready for it," I tell him. "I don't care if it hurts. I just want you inside me. Want you to take my virginity. Right now. Right here." I push myself up into a sitting position, and he comes with me. He such a sweetheart, but I see the raw hunger in his eyes. How much he's holding back. With trembling hands, I reach for him. I open his zipper, and stop breathing as his gigantic cock springs out.

## 8

*Ethan*

*I* must be dreaming. I only met my mate this morning. Now here she is, naked on my couch, her sweet thighs spread open, begging me to take her virginity.

She's so perfect, so tiny. But so wet. I stare at her swollen, pink pussy, mesmerized. Thinking how incredible it's gonna feel gripping my cock.

I'm not gonna rush this, though. I want to make sure everything is perfect for her.

She reaches out and closes her small, soft hand around the head of my dick. *Fuck.* I hiss out a groan of pure need.

She stares at it like she's fascinated. Pre-cum is already leaking out the head and, if I'm not careful, I'm gonna shoot my load right here. Come all over her lovely tits.

No, not happening. The first time I come is gonna be inside her. I'm gonna flood her womb with my seed.

When she runs her hand up and down the length of it, I clench my jaw, my body quaking with the effort of holding back.

"What's that?" she asks. She's so goddamn adorable.

"It's pre-cum, honeybun," I growl.

"Can I—?" She doesn't finish the sentence. Instead, she dips her head and licks it.

Holy shit. I tip my head back before my eyes roll back in my skull. This little angel is flicking her tongue over the head of my dick and making sounds like it tastes good. I don't dare look at what she's doing, because if I do, she's gonna be swallowing the whole load. Her tongue keeps licking, then I feel the softer sensation of her lips encircling the head. A little suction, and my cock is sliding into her sweet, warm cave. She moves back and forth, trying to get me in deeper. She's never done this before. Never been with a man before. She's doing all this on instinct. And it's beautiful.

At last, I open my eyes and look down at the sight of Jessica's mouth open wide, coping with my monster cock. My balls are aching, dying for a release. I pull out fast. She looks up at me, eyelids heavy, and reaches for me, pulling me down into a deep kiss. As her tongue plunges into my mouth, I marvel at how passionate she is, my beautiful sexy mate.

"I need you inside me, Ethan," she mutters against my mouth. "I'm aching so bad for you."

I slide my hand down and cup her pussy lips. I

swear she's even wetter than before. Her virgin juices are just about dripping down her sweet thighs. I cast around the cabin. The couch is real comfy. But I don't want her first time to be on a couch. My princess deserves something better. My gaze alights on the fire. I imagine its heat warming her lovely skin as my cock plunges into her. There's a cream, furry rug on the floor. It's perfect.

I sweep her up in my arms, carry her over to it and lay her down. Her legs fall open naturally, revealing her pussy to me. She might be a virgin, but she's not shy, my sweet mate. And I love that about her. One of the many things I love about her.

I arch over her again, kissing her deep until she moans into my mouth. Her small fingers dig into my shoulders and she writhes beneath me. She's ripe to be mated. Her lovely, lithe body so ready to bear my young. Leaning back, so I can savor every precious moment of this, I spread her thighs a little wider, then I press my swollen cock to her tight little opening. Damn. She's even tighter than I expected. I'm barely half an inch in when she cries out, pain marring her lovely features.

"Easy." I pull back, give her time to get used to me. I feel her clench around me as I ease in again, bumping up against the precious cherry that's about to be gone forever.

Her whole body is tense, but she's still deliciously wet and slippery.

"I'm gonna take your virginity right now," I growl in her ear.

"Yes, please take it, Ethan," she gasps. "I want it to be yours."

A growl of need breaks from my throat, my hips jerk involuntarily, and she gives a loud cry.

But a second later, her feet hook around my thighs and pull me in. "Just do it. I want all of you inside me," she gasps out. She's strong. Tiny, but fierce.

And I do it. With one clean, true thrust, I tear right through her virginity. Push my cock all the way home. I feel her tiny pussy spasm around my dick, hot and torn, and she whimpers.

"Don't worry, baby." I pepper her face with kisses. "It's gonna feel real good from now on." I give her a few moments to get used to me, then I give a tiny pump, and another one.

"Oh!" she cries out, and I feel her tension ease. A growl escapes my lips. She's ready.

I arch over her and start to fuck her. With every thrust, she gasps, her cherry red lips falling wide open. It's beautiful to see her like this. Wild, uninhibited.

I feel like I know her body already. This is all so new, but it feels like we're meant to be together. Like we fit each other perfectly. She has a tiny pussy, and I have a monster cock, but somehow, it's buried all the way inside her, my balls pressing up against her body.

"Ethan, you're going to make me come—" The end of her sentence is cut off by a loud cry, and her little pussy spasms around me.

*Fuck.* She's coming all over my cock, and I feel like she's milking me; trying to squeeze the seed out of it.

My beast's canines bust through my jaws. It rises to

the surface, urging me to give her the claiming mark that will bond us together forever. My cock deep in her pussy, my teeth on her neck. I want nothing more than to give her this permanent sign that she's mine. She belongs to me—

But it's too soon. Reluctantly, I push my beast back.

Instead, my hips pound harder and harder, and she keeps coming, one orgasm rolling into another. She's incredible my girl. Insatiable. When she's finally done, all weak and panting for breath, my teeth graze her neck, and I let loose with a roar, flooding her womb with my hot seed.

The first time of many.

My beast settles inside me and euphoria fills my veins. I've claimed her.

I pull out of her slow, but she makes a face.

"You sore, baby?"

"Yeah." She touches a hand between her thighs and examines it. There's a trace of pink. My cream and her virginity mixed together.

"Not a virgin anymore," she says.

"You're sure not." I gather her up in my arms, and hold her against my chest. "Not a virgin anymore," I growl. "Because you're mine."

"Mine," she echoes sweetly in my ear and snuggles herself closer against my chest.

## 9

*Ethan*

Goddamn sunlight streaming through the window.

Usually, I love being awoken up by the morning sun. But for the first time in my life, I wish the sky was gray and the storm was still raging, so I could keep Jessica right here, in bed with me all day. Instead, patchy blue sky is showing through the curtains, and a ray of light is kissing my sleeping princess's cheeks. She's snuggled in beside me, her head nestled against the crook of my arm.

I don't remember falling asleep last night. At some point, when rain was still battering the windows and the fire had died down to glowing embers, I carried her through to the master bedroom and we continued what we'd started, all comfy in my big bed. Then we must've drifted off, with her all wrapped up in my arms.

I've got a feeling it's late. Guess I should get up, deal with the broken-down bus. But there's no way I'm going to get out of bed and miss a moment of this. I'm just gonna lie here, listening to the adorable sounds of Jessica's breathing. She looks peaceful, her lovely features relaxed. I sure hope I've brought some peace into her life. Some belief that her douchebag ex-boyfriend won't come looking for her. Well, he sure won't once I've dealt with him.

Yesterday was the most perfect day of my life. But it went so fast. And today she's going to want to catch up with her brother. I guess that's right. He obviously worries about her. So long as she comes right back here when she's done.

And if she doesn't... if she wakes up now and says she never wants to see me again—

*No!* My beast roars in pain.

She's mine. I saw the emotion in her eyes. Her vulnerability when she gave me her virginity.

Her eyelids flutter and I hold still, knowing that my face will be the first thing she sees.

She gives a sleepy sigh and blinks. One, two, three times, until, finally, her big brown orbs snap open and...

A smile spills across her face like the sun coming out from behind clouds. My heart bounds. It's the most beautiful thing I've seen in my life.

"Good morning, honeybun," I say.

"Good morning." She raises her arms above her head

and stretches joyfully, like a little kid. I love that she has this innocence in her, after all she's been through.

"How did you sleep?"

"Oh, I think that was the best sleep of my entire life."

"Comfy bed, huh?"

"Comfy bed mate." She snuggles closer, wrapping her arms around me.

I sigh in pleasure. I love the way she fits against me, like we're two pieces of a jigsaw puzzle.

"And you?" She frowns. "I hope I wasn't snoring? My brother used to tease me about it when we shared a room as little kids."

She *was* snoring quietly, like a little bear cub, and it was adorable. But I'm not about to embarrass her by telling her that.

"You can snore as much as you like, baby," I tell her instead.

She grins. "Let's see if you're still saying that in six months' time—" She breaks off, her cheeks going beet red. But my heart swells. I love that she's thinking six months ahead.

This girl is mine, forever. I can't wait to tell her so. But six months is a good start.

"Guess I should get up," she says.

"You got somewhere you need to be?"

"Not exactly. Just wondering if my brother's got my message yet."

"You want me to go check?" I pull back the covers and climb out of bed.

Her face goes still, and she looks me up and down.

There I am, standing buck-naked, a huge boner jutting out in front of me.

She bites her lower lip. "Later," she says, and she flicks the covers off of her.

A growl breaks from my throat as she displays her gorgeous naked body to my hungry gaze.

I don't need a second invitation. I spread her sweet thighs and dive right in.

Before long, she's crying out my name, while her tight little pussy is gripping my throbbing cock like it was made for me.

An hour later, I'm sitting at my old wooden table, between the couch and the kitchenette, and Jessica is cooking us breakfast at my stove. Wearing nothing but the T-shirt I gave her last night, and the panties she was wearing yesterday, which have been drying by the fire. They're pink with little bows at the sides, and every time I look at them, my cock gets so hard it hurts.

I watch the muscles in her lovely thighs flex as she stretches up to grab some sugar from an overhead cupboard. She seems at home here. I feel like she's always been here. Like there was never a time when this little cabin wasn't ours.

*Ours.*

The word warms me all the way through.

Yesterday I thought I'd always be alone. Today, I'm living here with my mate.

She hums as she stirs some pancake batter in a skillet. I was planning to make breakfast, but she insisted. *After all I've done for her*, she said. Poor girl; she has no idea that this was the absolute least I'd do for my princess.

She comes over, stepping lightly with her long, slender legs, and puts two plates, piled with pancakes, on the table.

One of the stacks is massive, and the other is about the right size for a tiny human.

"I wasn't sure how much you need to eat," she says.

"Oh, this is perfect," I say with a grin.

Her smooth forehead furrows. "Do you need to like, eat for two, because you've got a bear inside you?"

I laugh. "Yeah, I guess so. I've always had a big appetite—" I break off, worried she'll be repulsed by the thought.

"I think that's real sexy," she says in a shy voice, her hand skimming my shoulder as she slides into her seat.

My beast unfurls inside me. She's incredible, my girl. In less than a day, she's not only come to terms with the fact that I'm half animal. She *likes* it.

"Is your bear happy that we... you know?" She's looking down now, picking at her food, but her cheeks are bright pink.

"Oh, you have no idea," I growl.

Her dark eyelashes flutter. "So, are we, like dating now?"

A laugh of surprise bursts out of me. "Dating? We're together. You're my mate. Don't you know that?"

"I-I wasn't sure if you meant just for the night."

"You would've mated me for just one night?"

She looks confused. "I mean, that wasn't what I wanted. But I couldn't stop myself. I just wanted to be with you. When I woke up this morning, I was worried it was just some kind of fantasy, because we were trapped here by the storm and all." Her words come out in a rush, and tenderness washes through me.

"Oh, honeybun. You're mine. I knew the second I laid eyes on you. It happened just like my grandad told me it would. And every moment I've spent with you has just made the feeling stronger. I want to hold you in my arms forever. Keep you here in my cabin and fill your belly with my young."

I see her throat constrict as she swallows hard.

"I know that's a lot to hear right now."

"N-no, I think I feel it too—" she stammers. She's scared to show her emotions, but so brave, my girl. She deserves everything I can give her and more.

"I'm falling for you, Jessica. Big time. You're more perfect than I imagined in my wildest dreams."

"Oh, I'm falling for you, too," she whispers.

Warmth fills my chest and my bear bounds in joy. I'm silent while I absorb this incredible news. It's time to tell her.

"I'm gonna give you my mark," I say.

"Your mark?" she echoes.

"When it's time. On the back of your neck."

"Oh—" She lifts her hand to the spot where I almost marked her several times already. "I remember... your teeth." She gives a small smile. "I thought you were giving me a hickey."

"It'll be way better than a hickey," I growl. "It won't turn purple and fade after a few days. It'll be there always. Show the whole world you're my property."

Her eyes get very bright. "I-I like that," she says slowly. I hear a catch in her breath, and the tell-tale perfume of her arousal drifts to my nostrils.

*Damn.* It took all my self-control to not give her my mark last night. And now, she's practically asking me for it.

My beast surges inside me, and before I can stop myself, I snatch her up from her seat and pull her onto my lap. I nuzzle her neck, inhaling her sweet, pure scent. *Damn.* I'm dying to possess her. Sink my cock all the way home, and give her my mark right now.

I pepper her soft neck with kisses, and she sighs and shivers, and whispers my name. It's fucking delicious.

"Why didn't you give me your mark last night?" she gasps out.

"I thought it was too soon. I want to make sure you're ready for it."

She draws back, cups my rough old face in her delicate hands and fixes me with a serious look. "Ethan, I'm ready for it, trust me. I'm a lot tougher than I look."

She is. I already know that about her. But she's so beautiful. So human. But I'm worried she needs more than living as the partner of a solitary bear.

She frowns. "What is it?"

"I'm a beast, and you're human."

She tilts her head to the side. "A human whose destiny it was to find a shifter mate."

I grin. I can't argue with that.

"I want all of you, Ethan. Man, beast, everything."

My bear lets out a purr; a deep, rolling sound of satisfaction.

"Show me," she says. Her voice is hoarse with desire, and I can't hold back any more. I kiss her long and fierce, plunging my tongue deep into her mouth. And she takes it all, sucking on it, tangling her fingers in my hair. I hold her tight, running my arms up and down her lovely body, then she shuffles around, and lifts her leg until she's straddling me.

Holy hell. The heat of her pussy is spilling through her panties, and my jeans. And she's grinding back and forth, like she's hungry to have me inside her again. I slide my hand down the front of her panties. So wet and soft and tight, clenching around my fingers—

A sound comes from outside.

My head snaps up. What's that?

A shuffling, grating sound of feet, coming from the forest and striding down my pathway.

Then someone knocking on my door with the flat of their hand. *Bang-bang-bang.*

They'd better have a darn good reason for disturbing us right now, or I'm gonna tear them a new one.

I ease Jessica off my lap. "Go out the back," I tell her.

She hurries off, not stopping to ask why. Because she trusts me.

I wait until she's out of sight, then I stride to the door and snatch it open.

Two shotgun barrels are pointing right at me.

Behind them is a man. A human, late twenties, dark hair and eyes, olive skin, determined expression. Jessica's brother. There's a distinct family resemblance.

"Put your hands up," he snarls.

I go to tear the gun from his grasp and knock him to the ground.

Then I stop, let my hand drop. He's the brother of my mate. First impressions and all. She won't be happy if I humiliate him; make an enemy of him. And her happiness is what I care about, more than anything.

I raise my hands casually. "No need for all that. Let's go inside and meet each other all civilized."

He sneers, his gaze raking me up and down. "Civilized. Right."

My bear growls. He's on thin ice. But I respect the guy's guts, his loyalty to Jessica.

"Jessica!" he bawls, trying to peer into the cabin. "Get out here!"

"She'll come when she's ready," I tell him. "And she's not gonna be happy to see you waving that gun at me."

There's a waft of air behind me, and her scent hits my nostrils. "Ricky! What on earth are you doing?"

Jessica appears at my side and I wrap my arms around her protectively. He might be her brother, but no one waves a gun near my mate.

"For the last time, put the gun away," I tell him.

He pales. My bear is rising up beneath my skin, the bones in my skull broadening, and I know he sees it.

He lets the shotgun fall to his side. "Jessica, what the

hell are you doing here, with this… this…beast?" he almost spits.

"Don't you dare talk about him like that!" Jessica yells.

I gaze at her in awe. Her voice is so strong, so confident. *My mate.* Pride surges in me.

And her next sentence takes my breath away:

"He's my mate, Ricky."

He shakes his head hard. "Your what?"

"My mate. I'm his. We're fated to be together."

The poor guy looks like he's about to combust. I almost feel sorry for him.

"Jessica, what the fuck? After all that bullshit with Kevin. After everything we've been through. Now this?"

He chokes out the last word. He's a man at the end of his tether. I remember Jessica saying he's been struggling to get his business started up again in a new town. Guess he's feeling pretty desperate right now.

"Listen," I cut in. "I know this is a lot to hear. Things happened real fast yesterday. But I'm in love with your sister. And I'm going to take care of her for the rest of her life—"

His eyes bulge. "If you've done anything to her, I'll kill you!"

"Ricky, it's not like that. I'm in love with Ethan, too," Jessica blurts out.

My head snaps to her and we exchange a long look. My heart pounds. All I want is to take her in my arms and kiss her senseless.

"Jessica, come with me, right now," Ricky grits out.

Her attention darts to me, and back to him again.

"Ethan, I'd better go. He needs a little time," she says, her voice dragging with regret.

I bunch my fists. My bear is whining, scrabbling, begging me to make her stay.

Letting her go is going to kill me.

And if she leaves now, she might not come back.

## 10

*Jessica*

"Ricky, you don't understand. And quit dragging me!" I tear my hand out of his grasp.

"Sorry, sorry." He shoots me a pained glance over his shoulder. "I'm just worried the storm's gonna come back."

I think he's right. The sky has turned an ominous gray again, and the air is full of static.

"All the more reason to have stayed in our cabin," I retort.

"Our!?" Ricky slams on the brakes. "What is this, our? You only just met this... this guy, Jessica. Are you out of your mind?"

He starts up again, striding so fast along the forest

trail that I have to jog to keep up. My jeans are still a little damp and hella uncomfortable. Luckily I tugged them on when I realized Ricky had come for me, so he didn't have to know that I've been walking around in my underwear.

"I know it sounds crazy—" I pant.

"We'll discuss this when we're home."

He's right. I need to save my breath for getting the hell out of here. It will really suck if we get caught in another deluge. I stare at his uncompromising back view as I follow after him. I kinda get where he's coming from. Things have happened so fast with Ethan. And the last time I met a guy, we wound up having to move towns and basically hide ourselves away like we were in witness protection. But Ricky doesn't need to treat me like I'm some naïve idiot. Yes, I failed to spot that my ex was a psychopathic weirdo until it was too late. But at the same time, I didn't fully trust him. I never went past first base with him. I always had this *feeling* that I wanted to wait until I met the right one, and I knew that wasn't him.

But with Ethan, everything is different. Every single moment with him has been so right. From our first conversation on the bus, to the way we woke up this morning in each other's arms. I don't have a single doubt about him, because he's my mate. The one I was fated to be with.

But how to explain that to my wired brother?

The sky is grumbling as we exit the forest, but there's Ricky's battered old sedan waiting for us in a small parking lot.

I feel a burst of gratitude toward him for looking out for me… which lasts all of ten seconds.

"You know what this guy is, Jessica?" he barks as he starts up the car.

I sigh. "Do you?"

Rain starts coming down, and he flicks on the wipers. Like the rest of the car, they're worn-out and they squeak back and forth unevenly.

"Yup, he's basically an animal. An animal with a human face."

"Don't you dare talk about him like that!" I yell, protectiveness pouring through me.

Ricky throws me a look of surprise. Guess my voice doesn't usually sound so fierce and kinda growly.

He shakes his head. "Okay, Jessica, tell me what's so great about this guy, that after one night together, you're ready to move in with him."

"He took care of me."

He grunts. "I hate to think what would've happened if I hadn't arrived just then."

Well, we would have had mind-blowing sex, that's what. But if I tell Ricky that, he'll never be able to look me in the eye again.

"He was looking after me, Ricky, can't you understand that? I was on the bus. The bus broke down and I took a shortcut through the forest, but a tree came down. I think it got struck by lightning, and he was right there, saving me."

"Right there?" His voice is dripping in sarcasm. "So, he followed you all that way?"

"Yeah, he did, but not in the way you think."

His lip curls in disgust. "One stalker wasn't enough for you, Jessica?"

"Ricky stop being such an ass. He saved me from being killed. If he hadn't been there, I'd be squished right now."

He has the grace to flinch.

"Then he took me back to his cabin. I had a shower in his real nice, modern bathroom. Nicer than the one we have here. Then he cooked me dinner... And we got to know each other a little better," I finish, glossing over some of the most pertinent details.

"I hope that's not a euphemism, Jessica," he growls.

"Ricky, I'm an adult. Please try to remember that. Ethan is..." I close my eyes. "He's the best thing that ever happened to me. And we're in love."

"Love?" Ricky screeches to a halt in front of our house, and I jerk forward, the seatbelt cutting into my shoulder. He grabs his shotgun off the backseat and stalks inside. Reluctantly, I go after him, my feet sloshing in the mud.

"AND WHAT WAS that lie you told me about staying in Brookville?" He rounds on me as soon as we're inside. "I got that message about a second before I checked your location on *find my phone* and discovered that you're right in the middle of the freaking forest."

"I didn't want you to worry. I knew there wasn't much coverage and I wouldn't have many chances to communicate with you. It just seemed simpler."

"Well, I was worried. I thought something awful had

happened to you, Jessica." His voice breaks. "You're all I've got. Don't you know that?"

I go still. "And you're so important to me, Ricky. I'm so grateful for all the sacrifices you've made for me."

A smile flickers on his lips. But then his face hardens again. "And that's why I'm not going to stand here and watch while you throw your life away on a beast—"

*Roaarrr!*

An awful sound tears through the air. The grunt of a powerful engine.

Ricky snatches up his shotgun again. "Is that him?" he demands, his eyes wild.

"I-I don't think so. He didn't mention owning a motorcycle."

"Right," Ricky says drily. "That didn't crop up in the less-than-twenty-four hours you spent together?"

"Ricky, I don't think it's Ethan. I think it's—"

There's another roar, and another and another.

Ricky peers through the curtain covering the living room window. "What were that asshole's colors like?" he demands.

"Kinda burnt orange and turquoise."

"That fucking prick's found you. Just like you said he would. But he hasn't come alone."

"Let me see." I run after him. He tries to shove me back, but I sneak under his arm and peek through the curtain, too.

The closest biker pulls off his helmet and my stomach plummets as I take in a familiar narrow face and cleft chin. My psycho ex. Whose right hand is sliding inside his jacket.

"It's him, and he's got a gun. They all have."

My heart jumps into my mouth as six bikers draw their guns and storm toward our flimsy wooden front door.

"Fuck, Ricky, what are we going to do?" I hiss.

Ricky cocks his shotgun, balances it on his shoulder. "Blow their fucking heads off, that's what." He dives to the front door and pulls back the latch.

"Ricky, no!"

He opens the door a crack and shoves the barrels of the shotgun through. "You come any closer and I'll take you all out!" he screams.

"You and whose army?" Kevin, my ex-boyfriend sneers. "You're all alone in there, aren't you? You and my old lady."

*Old lady?* My blood boils.

"I mean it!" Ricky screams. He's scared. He's never killed anyone before, of course.

"Get the hell out of here," I yell. "The only way I'm coming with you is if I'm dead."

Kevin gives a nasty laugh. "You know what I told you, Jessica. If I can't have you, no one will—"

*Boom!* The door smashes open. Ricky shoots, but he's knocked off his feet and the pellets spray the ceiling. I scream as my ex-boyfriend charges in. For a split-second he stills, and looks me up and down, a smile flickering on his lips.

And then he's got me in a headlock, his other arm tight around my waist. I kick and thrash with my elbows. He grunts in pain, but he doesn't let go. I watch in a dazed horror as his buddies stream through the door as well. The last one in aims a vicious kick at Ricky's stomach. Ricky crumples to the ground, but he keeps kicking him again and again.

"Stop!" I scream. "Okay, I'll come with you. Just don't hurt him."

"See?" Kevin breathes in my ear. "It doesn't have to be hard. Just do what I tell you, and you and me are gonna be real happy."

I let my body go limp and heavy as he drags me toward the door. I'm not about to make it easy for him.

He lets go of my waist, and reaches for the door knob... and the door smashes back against the wall.

A huge, dark figure fills the doorway. A grizzly bear-shaped figure, standing up on its back legs, claws and teeth flashing.

Then it parts its massive jaws and *roars*. It's an incredible sound, like a sonic boom, knocking everyone backwards.

Everyone except me.

Because, for me, it's the most welcome sound in the world.

The call of my mate.

I shove Kevin away from me and I stand on my two feet, locking eyes with Ethan. Love and admiration pour through me as I see him in his animal form for the first time. His fur is chocolate brown and glistening with health. His four massive feet are tipped with shining gray claws, and his teeth are gleaming white. His ears are pricked up and his eyes... his eyes are the ones I love. Emerald green and glowing with love and desire, for me. My heart pounds and we share a long look.

There's no need to speak; we understand each other perfectly.

Then he crashes down on all fours, the floor shaking under his weight. Rage flares in his eyes as he sweeps the room. He lets out a bellow, and he charges.

His huge bulk smashes right into Kevin. Kevin barely has time to scream before Ethan seizes his head in his massive jaws and hurls him at the living room wall. There's a loud thunk and Kevin slides to the ground in a crumpled heap.

The others start to flee to the kitchen, but Ethan is too quick for them. One after the other, he snatches them up, and shakes them until their brains rattle. Then he returns to Kevin. His eyes are glowing red with murderous fury.

I close my eyes. As much as I'd like to kill Kevin with my bare hands, I don't need to see this.

There's a slashing sound and a scream, and pleas for mercy.

A silence follows, then a muted crunching.

"Get him out of here," I hear Ethan's voice say. "And if any of you ever think about bothering these people again, you'll have the same treatment waiting for you."

There's some dragging and grunting and whimpers of pain. Then the front door slams shut.

At last, I open my eyes. The living room walls are dented in several places, the plaster's all cracked, and there's a small puddle of blood on the floor.

And there's Ethan, my mate, standing in the middle of my living room. Arms hanging loose at his sides, feet apart. Gloriously naked.

So big and powerful and sexy.

"Oh my god." I rush to him.

He clasps my hands briefly and plants a kiss on my forehead. "Just let me get dressed." He dives through the front door, and he's back in a moment, wearing his familiar jeans and wifebeater.

I run into his arms and press my head against his chest. "Thank you, thank you," I say. "Kevin was about to drag me away."

Ethan snarls and looks for Ricky, who's slumped against the wall.

"He did his best. But there were six of them, and they all had guns," I explain.

Ricky stands up, clutching his ribs and wincing. "Thanks," he mutters grudgingly. But I know my brother, and he's as impressed as hell.

"How did you know I needed help?" I murmur against Ethan's chest.

He cradles my head in his massive hands. "I told you I'd never leave you unprotected, Jessica. And I had a bad feeling after we saw those bikers yesterday. So, I followed you back here."

"But we were driving—" I break off. He ran on four paws. Of course, he did.

"You must've run like crazy." As I look up at the man I love, wonder spills through me.

He shrugs. "I don't remember it all that well. All I knew was I had to get to you."

"We're connected, aren't we?" I say. "You *knew* I was in danger."

"Right here." He presses my hand to his massive

chest again, and I feel the deep rumble that's already becoming so familiar to me.

"This is what being mates means."

He nods. "You're starting to get it."

I stare at him and a shiver goes through me as finally, I understand. It's not like boyfriends and girl-friends. It's so much more than that. Being mates means being completely connected to one another, like you share the same soul.

And right now, all I want is to be alone with my incredible mate, in each other's arms, reconnecting.

"Can we go back—?" I start to say, but a sound like a dying lawnmower starts up behind me.

Ricky is clearing his throat. Unsubtly. "I'm not real comfortable with this," he says.

Annoyance bubbles up in me. "You're still saying that, after Ethan just saved your ass?"

"No offence. I'm grateful and all for what you did." He sighs. "But Jessica, can't you find yourself a human boyfriend instead?"

I open my mouth to tell him it's none of his business, but Ethan lays his hand on my shoulder.

"I get it, bro. You're just trying to protect your sister, and that's admirable. But I'm in love with her. We're meant to be together."

Ricky goggles. "Are you going to go live in the forest, like some crazy mountain woman, and quit washing and shit? You had *ambitions*, Jessica."

I plant my hands on my hips. "Number one, Ethan has not one, but two showers at his cabin. And number two, he has wifi. Which is kinda important because he's an app designer."

Ricky plants his hands on his hips. "What have you designed?"

"You heard of Sick Rebellion?" Ethan says.

Ricky blinks several times. "You designed that?"

Ethan shrugs in that careless way of his. "Yup."

"No way!" His eyes look about ready to drop out of his head.

As Ricky starts jabbering on about how much he loves the game, I stalk off to the kitchen. Personally, I don't care whether Ethan's occupation is app designer, full-time mountain man, or bus driver. He's the smartest, most interesting, most protective guy I've met. But if that's what it takes to get Ricky onside…

Ten minutes later, I'm bringing three cups of coffee over to the coffee table. Ethan is showing Ricky some photos on his phone, and Ricky is nodding thoughtfully.

"Ricky thinks he can get hold of the parts I need for the bus. And fit them for me," Ethan says. "And if he's looking to branch out, I'm pretty sure the local bus service will give him more work than he can handle."

My heart leaps. "Ricky's a great mechanic," I say. "He had all five-star reviews at his last business."

"Four-point-nine," Ricky mumbles, but I can tell he's touched by my endorsement.

"Guess you need to get the show back on the road as soon as?" he asks Ethan.

Ethan spreads his hands wide. "Yup. Don't want to leave all those poor customers high and dry."

Ricky swigs back his coffee. "Let's go!" He jumps to his feet, then groans as his bruised body protests.

Ethan takes my hand and we exchange a look. He doesn't need to say anything—I understand. He's relieved that my brother is softening, because he knows it'll make me happy.

As we walk out to the car, Ethan wraps his arm around me and I swear I've never felt so protected in my life.

## 11

_Jessica_

*I*t's almost dark by the time we're hiking along the trail to the cabin. The storm has finally blown over, but the air is saturated and rainwater is dripping down from the trees. A lot has happened today, I think. Love, another near-death experience, and a beautiful new bro-mance. Also, Ricky managed to do a temporary fix on the bus, and he's ordered a replacement part from a buddy of his who has a junkyard full of ancient vehicles. And now the evening is stretching ahead of us and I can hardly wait.

"I need to clear out a track for your car, so you can drive right up here," Ethan says as he helps me over a fallen tree-trunk.

"Won't you hate that?" I say, gazing at the narrow trail that has been Ethan's route to civilization for years.

"I'll get used to it. Can't have my mate hiking through the forest every time you want to go someplace."

My breath catches. I love how much he's prepared to change for me. He already offered for us to move into the town, but I said no. I've got a feeling I'm going to love living in seclusion with him, surrounded by nothing but the sounds and smells of nature.

When the little cabin finally comes into view, my heart leaps. It looks so cozy and welcoming, like it's been waiting for us to come back.

"Welcome home, baby," Ethan murmurs, wrapping his arm around me and leading me to the front door. "This place is yours now. You can make any changes you want. Paint the front door, add some curtains, whatever makes you happy."

I'm so overwhelmed with happiness and excitement for our future, I suddenly feel like I can barely stand on my own two feet. Right on cue, Ethan sweeps me up into his arms. He kisses me long and deep, then he carries me over the threshold of our cabin.

*Our cabin,* I say to myself, over and over, and it feels so right.

When he's deposited me gently on the couch, Ethan excuses himself to start up the fire again, and in a couple of minutes, orange flames are leaping up from the pile of logs.

And then I'm back in his strong arms. Now we're alone again, I feel his wild, sexual energy unleashing itself. And, to my delight, I also sense his bear, pushing up against his skin. I love that it's showing itself to me, allowing me to connect with it.

He feels at my skin, checking my temperature. "You need a shower to get warmed up again?"

"Maybe..." I bite my lip as a mischievous thought pops into my head. "But you're not showering outside this time."

"No? Why's that?"

"Because you're showering with me."

Without waiting for him to respond, I tear my shirt over my head, and I start walking to the bathroom. My bra hits the floor next, then I shuck off my jeans, and by the time I open the bathroom door, I'm naked.

I haven't turned around, but I hear Ethan's sharp intake of breath. When I feel something hard pressing into my back, I know he's stripped his clothes off, too. Need burns through me.

"Don't turn around," he growls into the side of my neck. I do as he says, holding my arms by my sides and shivering in anticipation.

His hands come up and cup my tits. I love the way he pinches my nipples, making them ache like crazy. Then he takes hold of my hips and walks me toward the shower, prodding me with his erection. He turns on the water, and clouds of steam fill the room.

When his hand slides between my legs, I moan. I'm already wet for him. Already thinking how much I need that hard rod inside me. As we enter the shower, he keeps working at my pussy, spreading my wetness all over, teasing me with light touches. I lean back against his body as the hot water cascades all around.

He thrusts two fingers inside me and I start to pant.

"You wanna come like this?" he growls.

"Yes," I gasp out.

"Not happening." He withdraws his hand.

I make a sound of disappointment. "Why not?"

"Because you're going to come around my cock. I want to feel this little pussy milking the seed out of me." At last, he flips me around.

His cock is huge, swollen, pre-cum dripping out of the head. He lets me wrap my hand around it. When I stroke it up and down, his knees start to tremble. I love that I can affect him like this. It's so darn sexy, this huge, powerful man, quaking at my touch. Now it's my turn to tease him. I go slow, then fast, play with his balls a little. All the while, I watch the ecstasy and frustration playing out on his handsome face.

"Jessica—" he grits out.

In a moment, I'm swept up in his arms, pinned against the shower tiles, and his monster cock is forcing its way into my pussy.

So darn big. But now he's gotten my virginity, it goes in a little easier. He forces himself into me—little by little—until he hits home. I let out a wild cry. His whole cock is buried balls-deep in my pussy. Everything is hot and wet and slippery and delicious. We kiss hard and deep as he holds me in his arms and fucks me against the wall, while the water pours all around us.

"Feels so good, Ethan," I gasp.

"Just like fucking in a storm. But better. Because no way am I letting anyone get a look at this little body. It's mine now, Jessica, you understand that? Mine to fuck.

Mine to pleasure. This is the only cock you'll ever know."

He looks so wild and possessive, as he hammers me and hammers me. Ethan's cock is the only one I'll ever want, I think as my pussy spasms around his girth and I come all over him again.

When he eases me down to the ground, I gaze at his cock, confused. He hasn't come yet?

"I'm gonna take you to the bedroom." He turns off the shower, grabs a soft towel and dries me with it. I'm struck by how tender and patient he's being, when his whole body is trembling and twitching with need, and his cock looks fit to burst.

When he's satisfied that I'm perfectly dry, he dries himself off fast, then he takes my hand and leads me to the master bedroom. His cock is jutting out in front of him, like its raw power is leading us there.

I can feel myself trembling, too. I sense this is different. Something important is going to happen.

He lays me down on the comforter, and he spreads my thighs and stares at my pussy like he can't get enough of looking at it. Then he flips me onto my front and lifts up my hips. I arch my back for him. I have no idea what I'm doing, but it feels right.

His breath catches. "Fuck," he murmurs. "What a sight, honeybun."

I feel the tip of his cock running up and down, between my lips. "You want this inside you again?" he growls.

"Yeah," I gasp out. The feel of it is driving me crazy.

"Show me."

I shift my entrance to exactly the right spot and push back on it.

"That's it," he growls. "Grip my cock with your tiny pussy."

His fingers bite into my hips as he pushes himself into me. *Whoa*, it goes deep like this. His hips press down, pinning me against the mattress. Then he fucks me in long, powerful strokes. Arching over me like the fierce beast he is.

Suddenly, I feel his teeth, grazing the back of my neck. I stop breathing.

This is it. This is where he gives me his mark, so the whole world will know I'm his. We'll be permanently bonded.

"Give it to me," I gasp out. "I want your mark, Ethan. I want all of you."

He lets out a roar. The sound of his bear. Yearning pours through me. I want this more than I've wanted anything in my life.

And his teeth bite down. *Owww.* My eyes tear up as those sharp canines pierce my skin. But I don't pull away. I hold still, giving myself to him. At the same time, his cock pounds me harder. Pain and pleasure mingle in an incredible harmony. The back of my neck and my pussy are two epicenters of ecstasy, and every bit of me is alive to him. My mate, claiming me body and soul. Making me his, forever.

When he unleashes a roar and shoots his hot seed inside me, I'm ready for him. I orgasm around his ejaculating cock, again and again, until he's flooded my womb and we're both spent, perfectly in unison.

## 12

*Jessica*

"Well, I'll be damned! That old bus?" Ethan's grandad slaps his thigh and laughs until tears leak from the corners of his emerald-green eyes. "I knew it, I just knew it, Kiddo."

Ethan lets off a growl. "Less of the Kiddo, grandad. How many times?"

"Oh, I'm sorry." Norman pats his grandson's hand and throws me a wink. "He's always gonna be the baby of the family to me, no matter how big and burly and famous he is."

Ethan shakes his head. "Not famous. I design apps. That's all."

"One of the biggest sellers in the App store." Norman crooks one of his thick, gray eyebrows. "You know that, my dear?"

"I sure do." I reach for Ethan's hand, unable to resist a small smile. I can see that Norman is a handful, but the love between the two bear shifters is obvious.

Norman adjusts his position in the hospital bed and Ethan darts forward to help him. Apparently his hip is healing well after the operation and he should be home in a week or so.

"You can't imagine how grumpy he was when I asked him to take over the route," Norman says.

"Also not true," Ethan mumbles, staring at his feet. "I was happy to help."

"Oh, I know you're always ready to help out your old grandad. I also know you're not the most sociable guy in the world. But I just had a feeling…" Norman's eyes twinkle as he looks at me again. He holds out one of his massive paws and I take it. "Welcome to the family my dear. I'm so happy that Ethan has found you."

"Thank you," I say, and suddenly, I'm blinking back tears. I love the thought of being part of Ethan's big, rough and tumble family. All these years, it's just been me and Ricky. We've always looked out for each other, but I know we've both longed for a big, rowdy family. Now, Ricky is starting to warm up to Ethan, and I hope he'll soon get to know the others, too, so we can all hang out together.

The door of the room swings open and two huge men stride in, one carrying a big bunch of flowers and the other with a six-pack of beer tucked under his arm.

Ethan slides his arm around my waist. "Jessica, meet my brothers, Lucas and Noah."

Lucas strides forward, hand outstretched. "Good to

meet you, Jessica." He's the oldest of the three, I figure. He has a serious, straightforward look to him.

"Hey, Jessica." Noah shakes my hand next. "Heard a lot about you." He's the middle one, but somehow, he seems younger than Ethan. His eyes are full of mischief, and I've heard from Ethan that he's always getting into scrapes.

"It's so great to meet you guys," I tell them.

I see their eyes drift to the mark on my neck—the one Ethan gave me two days ago, which is still tingling. Something moves across their eyes—two identical looks of reverence—and I glow with pride. I love bearing Ethan's mark. He says it's international shifter language meaning *keep the hell off.* And even though these guys are his brothers, and he trusts them with his life, I can see the weight it carries.

We stay for a few minutes, chatting, until Norman insists we run through the whole story of how we met —again.

"I'll let you take over the reins, grandad," Ethan says, squeezing his shoulder. "You've always been a better storyteller than me."

We say our goodbyes, and I can hardly keep up with Ethan as he strides out of the building.

"Remember how I said my grandad was a bit of a character?" he says when we get back to the car. "Understatement of the century."

I grin. "He's pretty awesome."

Ethan groans. "When he's not embarrassing the hell out of me. He's real taken with you though."

"He is?"

"Totally. Didn't you see how happy he looked?" He puts his arms around me and holds me close.

"I guess," I mutter against his big, broad chest, while my stomach flutters with pure happiness.

"I can't believe he didn't get all, *I told you so* about the cabin though."

"Huh?" I lift my head and give him a questioning look.

"He gifted it to me, because he said I'd need a lot of space for my family. I didn't believe him, of course. But now…" Instead of finishing his sentence, he dips his head and draws me into an incredible, tender kiss.

He doesn't need to say any more. We've already talked about having kids and agreed that we both want to have a ton of them. There's a couple of things I want to do with my life first, but to be honest, I can't wait to get started growing Ethan's cubs in my belly.

\* \* \*

"WHERE ARE WE GOING?" I ask Ethan a few days later. His grandad is back driving the bus, and Ethan has plenty of time on his hands now, so he's taking me on a mystery trip.

He grins from the driver's seat of his truck. "You'll see."

I fold my arms and snort a little bit. *Sheesh.* I've been the mate of a bear for two weeks and I'm already acting like a grizzly. Well, I kind of like it. I love how shifters are so direct and don't hide their feelings in a lot of complicated human bullshit.

As we drive all the way up to Brookville, my curiosity grows. But then he pulls up in front of the Jewelry Workshop.

"Ethan, what are we doing here?" I shoot him a panicked look. "You're not going to beat the crap out of him, are you?"

Okay, there *was* a tiny, tiny part of me that wanted to see my sleazy boss get his just desserts, but that was days ago. Now I'm so dang happy and in love, I don't give a damn.

Ethan raises my hand and presses it to his lips. "Nope. I promise you, I'm not going to hurt him."

"So, what are we doing here?"

"Starting your internship, of course. You just go in like normal, and I'll follow. You don't need to worry about me."

"I don't know about this," I mutter, as I climb out of the truck, but curiosity is already getting the better of me.

Ethan stays right behind me as I ascend the three flights of stairs to the workshop. When I fling open the door, my boss, Christopher, is sitting behind his desk.

Surprise and pleasure cross his face as he takes me in. "Jessica! You decided to come back after all—"

He freezes, the color draining out of his face.

"I'm Ethan," my gorgeous mate says, stepping forward and pushing up the sleeves of his shirt. "Jessica's partner. When she told me about the first day of her internship, it sounded so awesome, I thought I'd swing by and see if you've got space for another intern."

Christopher's mouth falls open, and I dart a look at

Ethan. He wants to be a student here? Surely he's joking. But the expression on his face is perfectly calm.

"A-another intern?" Christopher splutters.

"You won't need to worry about me, I'll just sit over there." Ethan tilts his chin toward a desk in the far corner of the room. "And when you've got a spare minute, you could give me a few pointers."

My boss's mouth works silently.

Ethan plants his hands on his hips and takes another step closer. "Or maybe you only take beautiful young women as interns?"

I bite down on my tongue to stop myself from laughing.

"N-no, as it happens I-I do have a place available for all genders. For you," Christopher chokes out.

"Good." Without waiting for any further invitation, Ethan saunters across the room and takes a seat behind the desk. "Ready when you are, boss."

It's an 'interesting' morning. My boss is so nervous, he can hardly string a sentence together, while Ethan is acting like there's nothing unusual about him gate-crashing my internship. While I... I'm so full of love and gratitude, I'm glowing all over.

"I THINK I'll be fine by myself now," I tell Ethan on the second morning.

He frowns. "No way am I leaving you alone, Jessica."

And he's as good as his word. He drives me to work every morning, and stays with me all day long. Sitting in the corner, watching over me while he works on some mysterious piece that he refuses to show to me.

And the weird thing is, after the initial awkwardness fades away, the internship goes really well. My boss tries so hard not to look at me, it's comical. But aside from that, he's a good teacher, and I make a ton of progress.

It's fun working with a master craftsman, while my big, growly mate sits only feet away from me. Every couple of hours we take a break, and we usually spend it strolling the streets of Brookville or making out in the truck.

I love our weekday routine. Out all day, then back home to our lovely cabin before the sun sets.

And as soon as we're home, Ethan lights the fire, and we strip off and greet each other as nature intended. There's no need for clothes when I'm with my big, sexy bear. All it takes is a touch or a kiss and he's ready for me.

Ready to remind me who I belong to.

Again and again and again.

# EPILOGUE

*Eighteen months later*

"*I*s it nap time yet?" I ask, turning my back to Jessica.

"One pair of eyes fully closed, the other pair... drooping," she says of the two little heads that are resting on my shoulders.

"Oh, yeah. Definitely nap time." I follow her to the rear of the cabin, and very carefully, we lay our twins down in the bedroom they share. It's a super-cute little room, done out in yellow and sea-green, and I painted a bunch of little creatures of the forest all over the walls.

Caleb carries right on sleeping, while his sister is fussier. Jessica strokes her soft baby forehead until she relaxes into sleep. She's such a great mom. A natural. She does everything on instinct. The news that our firstborn was actually going to be two babies didn't faze her one bit. *Double the love*, she said.

We creep out on tiptoes, closing the door softly.

Back in the kitchen, we let out contented sighs. Getting our two babies to nap in sync is an achievement.

Usually, I love this time of day. Jessica and I try to get our work done in the mornings, while sharing childcare duties, so, when the twins go for their nap, we have some time for each other. But they're teething at the moment and it feels like we haven't spent enough time together recently.

I flick on the kettle to make some tea, then lean back against the counter. "What time are my brothers coming over, again?"

"Six," she tells me, propping her sweet ass on the edge of the kitchen table. She's breathtaking, in a yellow button-down sundress. I'm already getting hard at the thought of stripping it off her. Eighteen months and two babies later, and everything still feels brand-new and as exciting as the day I took her virginity. Around her neck, she wears the pendant that I made for her during her internship. It's nothing like as good as the jewelry that she makes nowadays, and sells for a bomb in her online store, but I'm so touched that she wears it every day, instead of one of her own pieces. Just one of the many ways she shows me she loves me.

"Ah. Plenty of time, then," I say.

"For what?" she asks innocently, but her gaze darts to my crotch, and she's biting her lower lip in that way that means she's thinking about us getting naked.

"For at least three orgasms."

She tilts her head to the side. "How's that going to happen?"

*Damn.* I love it when she acts all clueless and virginal. It sends my beast into overdrive.

"Well." I stalk over to her, slowly, deliberately. "First of all, I'm going to undress you…" I press my lips to her sweet mouth, at the same moment that my hands close around her tits. She's still breast-feeding and they're tender, but I know how to be gentle with them.

I unfasten the buttons on the front of her dress, then I unhook her bra, and her breasts come free.

My breath catches. "So sexy," I mutter. I love her body even more since she's given birth. It has pretty much gone back to how it was before, except that her tummy is softer, and her tits are huge, with darkened nipples. I kiss and lick them, before reaching for her panties.

She's wet already. Drenched. A groan of need breaks from my throat as I slide them down her thighs and fall to my knees in front of her. I spread her lovely thighs and drink in the sight of her beautiful pink pussy. Then I dive right in. Her scent is intoxicating, like the smell of night flowers, and I can't get enough of it.

I lick her slit, teasing and teasing until she tugs on my hair in frustration.

"Ethan, I need to come already!" she hisses out. I smile to myself as she moves me exactly where she wants me and grinds her little bud against my face.

I latch onto her clit just how she likes it, and in a less

than a minute, her whole body is quaking like a volcano that's about to blow.

The moment she's done, all weak and breathless, I flip her around and bend her over the kitchen table. She arches her back for me, and I take a moment to enjoy this perfect view of her sweet pussy and pink little rosebud, before I plunge all the way in in a single thrust.

Her pussy is still spasming from her orgasm, and I feel her clench around me as I thrust.

"So darn tight, honeybun," I grunt out. "So wet and sexy."

She gives a wild moan.

Then she goes limp as a ragdoll, while I screw her over the table, just how she likes it—sweet and wild and a little bit dirty.

I fuck her and fuck her, and she comes twice more, gripping the edge of the table and crying out my name in that sweet voice of hers.

I can't hold back any more. "You want me to come inside you?" I say.

"Yes… no!" she yells in a sudden panic.

I grin and pull out of her. "Good job, because you're as fertile as hell right now," I say, as I shoot my load all over her gorgeous ass.

She sighs in pleasure as I rub my seed into her silky skin.

"No more babies. At least for another year," she mutters.

"Deal." I turn her around and pull her into my embrace. "But next time, I think we should shoot for triplets."

She gasps and gives me a dirty look.

"Kidding." I laugh and press my lips to her forehead. I've been teasing her that multiple births are common among shifters. "As long as we wind up with at least six overall."

"Done." She tugs my head down for a kiss. "And you better let me know when I'm fertile."

"I swear."

She narrows her eyes. "Or no more sexy times until I'm ready to conceive."

"Like you could hold out that long," I tease.

For a moment, she looks outraged. Then she checks the clock on the oven and bites her lower lip. "You think we have time to go again?"

I push her thighs apart and insert myself between them. "Definitely."

THE END

# READ THE OTHER BOOKS IN THE SERIES

If you like fated-mate romances, with plenty of V-card fun and tons of feels, check out the other books in the series at:

**arianahawkes.com/obsessed-mountain-mates**

# READ MY OTHER OBSESSED MATES SERIES

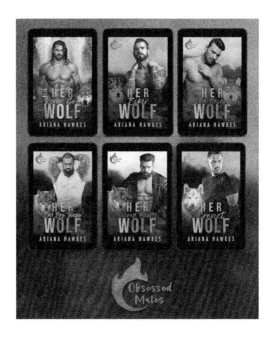

If you like steamy insta-love romance, featuring obsessed, growly heroes who'll do anything for their mates, check out my Obsessed Mates series. All books are standalone and can be read in any order.

**Get started at arianahawkes.com/obsessed-mates**

# READ THE REST OF MY CATALOGUE

**MateMatch Outcasts: a matchmaking agency for beasts, and the women tough enough to love them.**

★★★★★ "A super **exciting, funny, thrilling, suspenseful and steamy shifter romance series**. The characters jump right off the page!"

★★★★★ "**Absolutely Freaking Fantastic**. I loved every single word of this story. It is so full of **exciting twists that will keep you guessing until the very end** of this book. I can't wait to see what might happen next in this series."

Ragtown is a small former ghost town in the mountains, populated by outcast shifters. It's a secretive place, closed-off to the outside world - until someone sets up a secret mail-order bride service that introduces women looking for their mates.

**Get started at arianahawkes.com/matematch-outcasts**

# MY OTHER MATCHMAKING SERIES

My bestselling *Shiftr: Swipe Left For Love* series features Shiftr, the secret dating app that brings curvy girls and sexy shifters their perfect match! Fifteen books of totally bingeworthy reading — and my readers tell me that Shiftr is their favorite app ever! ;-) Get started at arianahawkes. com/shiftr

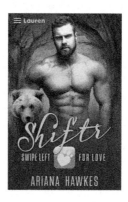

★★★★★ "**Shiftr is one of my all-time favorite series**! The stories are funny, sweet, exciting, and scorching hot! And they will **keep you glued to the pages!**"

★★★★★ "**I wish I had access to this app**! Come on, someone download it for me!"

**Get started at arianahawkes.com/shiftr**

# CONNECT WITH ME

If you'd like to be notified about new releases, giveaways and special promotions, you can sign up to my mailing list at arianahawkes.com/mailinglist. You can also follow me on BookBub and Amazon at:

bookbub.com/authors/ariana-hawkes
amazon.com/author/arianahawkes

Thanks again for reading – and for all your support!

Yours,
Ariana

* * *

USA Today bestselling author Ariana Hawkes writes spicy romantic stories with lovable characters, plenty of suspense, and a whole lot of laughs. She told her first story at the age of four, and has been writing ever since, for both work and pleasure. She lives in Massachusetts with her husband and two huskies.

www.arianahawkes.com

# GET TWO FREE BOOKS

**Join my mailing list and get two free books.**

 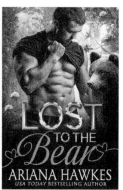

### Once Bitten Twice Smitten

A 4.5-star rated, comedy romance featuring one kickass roller derby chick, two scorching-hot Alphas, and the naughty nip that changed their lives forever.

### Lost To The Bear

He can't remember who he is. Until he meets the woman he'll never forget.

**Get your free books at arianahawkes.com/freebook**

# READING GUIDE TO ALL OF MY BOOKS

**Obsessed Mates**

Her River God Wolf

Her Biker Wolf

Her Alpha Neighbor Wolf

Her Bad Boy Trucker Wolf

Her Second Chance Wolf

Her Convict Wolf

**Obsessed Mountain Mates**

Driven Wild By The Grizzly

Snowed In With The Grizzly

Chosen By The Grizzly

**Shifter Dating App Romances**

Shiftr: Swipe Left for Love 1: Lauren

Shiftr: Swipe Left for Love 2: Dina

Shiftr: Swipe Left for Love 3: Kristin

Shiftr: Swipe Left for Love 4: Melissa

Shiftr: Swipe Left for Love 5: Andrea

Shiftr: Swipe Left for Love 6: Lori

Shiftr: Swipe Left for Love 7: Adaira

Shiftr: Swipe Left for Love 8: Timo

Shiftr: Swipe Left for Love 9: Jessica

**Shifter Holiday Romances**

Bear My Holiday Hero

Ultimate Bear Christmas Magic Boxed Set Vol. 1

Ultimate Bear Christmas Magic Boxed Set Vol. 2

Printed in Great Britain
by Amazon

39843732R00069